MARRIED TO A BROWNSVILLE BULLY: PART TWO

JAHQUEL J.

TEXT UCP TO 22828 TO SUBSCRIBE TO OUR MAILING LIST
If you would like to join our team, submit the first 3-4 chapters of your completed manuscript to
Submissions@UrbanChaptersPublications.com

A NOTE FROM THE AUTHOR –

Shout out to this being book #50! If you've been riding from the very first book – thank you for riding. If you're just now tuning in, welcome cousin! I personally loved writing the second book to this series. It got deep at some parts and then I got teary eyed at some parts. Now, I wish I was that author that could write one or two books and be done with a series. *Sighs* I'm not and my mind won't allow me to shut these characters up. I am trying my hand at standalones so we'll see how that goes. This series was supposed to be two books, and that changed. Quiet to all of you that told me it would change lol. Y'all know me so well. On the real, this book will be three books long and the third book is in the works. The release date for book 3 is at the back of the book. Thank you all so much for rocking with me and my team! We appreciate your support more than you'll ever know! Let me shut up so you can enjoy this book.

Warning: Don't hold your phone or any electronic devices – I am not responsible

www.facebook.com/JahquelJ
http://www.instagram.com/_Jahquel
http://www.twitter.com/Author_Jahquel
Be sure to join my reader's group on Facebook
www.facebook.com/ Jahquel's we reading or nah?

Erika, Jaleesa, Jaki, Jaya, and Saequan – True proof that my heart beats out of my chest.

YASHLIEGH – YASH – LEE
YOSHON – YO- SHAWN
YOLANI- YO- LA- NEE

1

Golden

I STOOD GRIPPING the wall as I stared at the man I married. The man that I went half on a baby with, and the same man who raped and beat me in front of our son. My heart was beating a mile a minute and I felt like I couldn't breathe. Grand had this smirk fixed on his face as his eyes went from Gyan to me. Gyan jumped down from the stool and ran right into my arms. Yoshon was confused and trying to read my face. He was trying to figure out what was going on? The tension in the room was so thick that Pit Pat's sharpest knife couldn't cut into this. She stood with her hand propped on one hip and the other hand gripping the handle of her knife. Grape stared at me confused, and I held my son tightly in my arm as I felt his tears wet my shirt.

"The fuck is going on? How you know Fear?" Yoshon turned toward me and questioned me.

"I... I gotta go," I backed out of the kitchen while holding onto Gyan like my life depended on it.

"Tell em, Golden. Why you acting shy now?"

"Acting shy!" I screamed. This man has tortured me and made my life a complete hell because of the shit he has done for me. Me sleeping in the car, working two jobs and trying to provide for my son all while being homeless in New York City was all his fault. He was the reason for this and he had the nerve to tell me to quit acting shy?

"You fucking raped and beat me, then left me for dead!" I screamed with tears streaming down my eyes. My hands were shaking and I couldn't even see straight. When I testified against this man, I thought I would never have to deal with him again. I went as far as to send him divorce papers to prison and never heard anything from him. It made me sick to my stomach to know that I was legally married to this man and that he wasn't worth the ground I walked on.

"Nah, what the fuck you just said?"

"Golden, why you putting on for these people? Huh? I didn't do shit to you. All I want to do is have a relationship with my son and you took that shit away from me."

"I didn't take anything away from you. You took that away from yourself when you decided that beating and raping your wife was the best choice you could make."

"Yoshon, what's good with this? You fucking with my wife now or something?" he switched subjects. Yoshon was calm... he was too calm.

"What she saying true?"

From the corner of my eye, I could see Grape getting prepared with his piece, and making sure he was near Pit Pat. "What the hell is all of this about? Gold, this man did this to you? Nonsense, you and Gyan are shaking and terrified. Yoshon, you do what you need to do, but you don't do it in or near our home, you hear?" Pit Pat gave him a stern warning.

I could tell he was in a tough spot. He had me, and Gyan huddled up in fear, and then he had his grandmother, who he didn't want to involve into anything. It was hard standing here and staring at Grand. He acted as if nothing happened and I was the one who was tripping. I knew what he did to me and so did my son. Any other little boy would have run right into his father's arms after seeing him for the first time in a little under a year. Instead, he took off running right into my arms and stared at his father like the monster he was.

"Look, I came to visit you and see what was up with Yolani. Last I spoke to her, she was supposed to get up with me and do business. When Grape invited me over, I thought I would catch up and talk business. As far as my fucking wife and son being here, how the fuck was I supposed to know I would walk into this?" He grabbed his car keys out his pockets.

"Grand, I'm not asking all that shit. Did you do that shit to her?" Yoshon asked once again and stared right into his eyes.

"Nigga, you think I'm into raping bitches? Shorty been after me since I asked for a divorce. Did she mention how the fuck she tried to kil—"

"You promised we would never bring it up!" I screamed. "After all you've put me through, that's the one thing you owe me," I cried with tears streaming down my eyes.

"Fuck all that shit. When you decided to get me arrested, run off with my money and my son, you broke all that shit. Want to know how perfect Golden is? She's always been good at saving face and trying to portray herself like she's the fucking victim. I'm the fucking victim!" he raised his voice, causing me and Gyan to jump. It was a loud roar that we had gotten accustomed to not hearing, and here he was again in the flesh, bringing us back down memory lane.

"Grand, leave... just leave!" I screamed.

Yoshon was trying to figure this all out. I could see from his laid-back demeanor that he was pissed and just wanted answers. "Nah, not until they know who the fuck is under their roof."

"Leave Dad!" Gyan called out.

"See. She got my own son turned against me. Bet he wouldn't be singing the same tune if he knew how you tried to kill him and yourself by doing damn near a hundred miles per house without him properly strapped to his seat. If that wasn't enough, the crazy bitch tried to drive off a fucking cliff with my son." He revealed a piece of my past I tried hard to forget every day.

Yoshon, Pit Pat, and Grape's expressions were one I wished I hadn't witnessed. You could see the judgment and shame all in their eyes as they avoided looking at me. While Pit Pat and Grape stared away, Yoshon stared at me, and I looked away. My heart was shattered and bruised.

"Is what he saying true, Golden?"

"Yosho—"

"Dead all that shit, is what the fuck he just said true?" he asked again, and I was at a loss for words. It's like I had a bunch of stuff being tossed around in my head, but I couldn't form a sentence.

"I'm 'bout to dip. Tell Yolani that I'm in town and need to see her about business. Make no sense I had to come up this way anyway," he mumbled and headed out the door.

We fought so hard to get away from him and we finally found a small piece of happiness. Yoshon made me happy, and Gyan was so happy being around Pit Pat and Yoshon. Then, Grand came in, snatched it away, then walked out the door. Every time I felt that I was making progress, I was always knocked back down to remind me that I didn't deserve happiness. The door closed, and I was stuck standing here with three people wanting to know answers.

"I'll go pack our things," I sobbed as I pulled Gyan up to my room. There was no need to sit here and try to fix things. The look on Yoshon's face told me everything I needed to know.

"Mom, do we have to go? Just go and talk to Mr. Yoshon," Gyan tried to convince me.

"It's much more complicated than that, baby. I'm so sorry

about what I'm putting you through. You don't know how much I love you, Gyan." I held his face and cried to him.

The door opened and Yoshon walked through the door. "Yo, Gee, go ahead and go finish eating," he told Gyan, and he stood by the door.

"You're not going to beat her up, right?" he asked in a shaky voice.

Yoshon's facial expression changed. "I would never put my hands on a woman. Real men don't hit women, you hear me?"

"Yes," he replied and left the room reluctantly.

I pulled things out the draws and placed them neatly on the bed. Yoshon sat in the chair in the corner and didn't say anything. He watched me closely as I prepared the clothes so I could pack them into my bag.

"Why?" was all that came out his mouth.

"Yoshon, if I told you my real story, would you have helped me? That was too much to lay on one person."

"You didn't fucking let me decide that. I told you upfront that I didn't like fucking liars and you continued to lie to me."

"I had to!" I cried. "You see my life. You see my husband; I didn't know if you knew him or not. Grand does a lot of business in New York and it was a risk I wasn't willing to take."

"Fucking lying to me is cool, though? Heard you." He stood up and headed to the door. "Like I said, I'm not a fucked-up nigga, so y'all staying here. When I got you, I got you." With that, he walked out the room door.

I wanted to scream, grab him and demand he hold me tight because I was scared. Yet, my legs stood there stuck like cement as I watched as he closed the door behind him. There was no need for tears because they were pouring down my eyes as I watched him leave the room. Yoshon had always kept it truthful with me and all he asked was for me to do the same, and I didn't. I lied about everything and thought that we could build something together. How stupid of me to think we could build something based on my lies. Plopping on the bed, I put my head in my hands and silently cried. Seeing the hurt on his face was enough to make me break down further. Why did shit like this always happen to me? I tried to be a good person, and I prayed and asked for forgiveness for all my sins. Why did things like this happen to always fall right into my lap? It was a question I spent years trying to figure out.

When Grand went across my face for the first time, I asked myself the same question. Instead of leaving, I continued to be there like a dummy. God was punishing me; he had to be. He sat there and pulled me out of situations I had no business being in, and I continued to rush my dumb ass right back into those very same situations. Just as I was about to stand up, Pit Pat came into the room. Staring down at the ground, I felt like I had let her down. She had welcomed me into her home and family with open arms, and the least I could do was be open and honest with her. Instead, I continued to lie to her and her grandson while living in their home.

"Pit P—"

"Save it, Golden. Now, I don't know what went on with that situation, but I do know you're scared of that man, and your child is scared of that man. He had the right name today because soon as he walked through that door, fear was written all over you and Gyan's face. I don't condone how you went about lying to us when we could have helped, but you're a mama on a mission and trying to protect your baby, so I understand. My grandson doesn't understand, and instead of trying to give him space, you need to go in there and make it right with him and explain your actions," she told me.

"He hates me, Pit."

She came over and sat next to me, pulling me into her arms. "Yoshon couldn't hate anybody. He may dislike you right now, but he doesn't hate you. You have made that man the happiest I've seen him since his fiancée died. Make this right, Golden." She kissed my forehead and held me for a bit longer.

"I'm sorry for all of this. You both have done so much for me, and in return, I lied and allowed you to believe I was someone that I wasn't."

"All that you've shown us is you. I believe you lied about your situation, but not about your characters, morals, and personality. You're a good woman and mother, and that's hard to lie about. Actions have always spoke louder to me than words, and that's what your actions have told me. Take some time to clean your face up, and then go and speak to him."

"Okay," I promised her. She kissed me once more and then headed out the bedroom. Once again, I was there with my thoughts, and they were running wild. Yoshon had been there for me when the world turned its back on me. He was the one to breathe life back into me and Gyan's life.

I should have told him about everything. Every time we were around each other I wanted to tell him about me running from my past demons. Each time I tried, it was like my mind went blank. It was as if I couldn't speak the truth and more lies spilled out my mouth. Yoshon didn't deserve me. I had too much baggage for him, and he deserved someone who loved and cared for him. Eva was the woman for him and I planned to tell him that when I went to apologize. If it was up to me, I would have stayed cooped in this room for the entire day. Pit Pat made me promise, and I didn't want to let her down by not going to speak to him and make things right. My defense mechanism was to back up and run from any situation that I didn't want to deal with. I could have stayed and faced Grand when he was released from prison, except I didn't. I decided to take my son and run far away from this man.

I leaned back on the bed and sighed a breath of frustration. Pit Pat had spoken through the intercom and told me that she was going to take Gyan to school this morning. Turning over on my side, I closed my eyes and let a tear escape from my eyes. Why did Grand have to come and fuck up the small piece of happiness I had in my life? For once, I was finding that smile that I hadn't seen in close to a year, and he comes in and snatches it away in under a minute. Then, he had the nerve to lie and place the blame on me. As a wife, I was there for him through everything. Even with all the shit he put my ass through, I was still there waiting with a clean home, hot meal and a kid that was well taken care of. Grand didn't have to do a damn thing when it came to Gyan. I taught him everything he knew and went to every doctor's appointment without him. When he first found out that we were expecting a son, he was over the moon.

Here I was smiling and thinking I was hot shit because I had Fear, one of the biggest kingpins in Virginia's baby in my stomach. Not to mention, it was his first son, so I was gloating as I pushed my Range Rover around and totted that big ol belly of mine around. Bitches hated me and cut their eyes whenever they seen me around. Still, I smiled and ate all that shit up because I was his one and only. Little did they know, the same Fear that everyone loved in the streets was a damn monster behind closed doors. I've seen this man treat the homeless better than he treated me and his son. We were just leeches who used his money to survive. It was no surprise when he started fucking around with the same bitches that were once jealous of me. So, I went from being envied to being pitied. These bitches weren't jealous of me anymore; they pitied me instead.

Putting my hands over my face, I sighed loudly and put a pillow over my face. All of this was too much, and I needed a minute to myself. I promised Pit Pat I would go and speak to Yoshon, and I would. Right now, I just needed a moment to myself before I did.

2

Yoshon

I woke up and saw Eva staring at me like she was a fucking nut case. Turning over, I pulled the covers over my head, but that didn't stop her. Instead, she continued to sit there and mumble shit under her breath. There was a million places I could have went to, instead my wheels stopped at Eva's apartment. Something told me that I should have just pulled the fuck off, but my dick told me I needed to take my anger out on something. Since I wasn't fucking with Golden's lying ass right now, I ended up here with Eva, and now I was regretting that shit. I had shown up a little after I left Golden's room and spent the entire day here. Yeah, we fucked, and I took my frustrations out on her pussy. She kept trying to kiss and make it shit that it wasn't. All I wanted was to bust this nut and hit that pussy from every angle as possible while I thought about Golden. Grabbing my phone off the nightstand, I noticed I had six missing calls from Grape.

"Why you staring at me like that?" I pulled myself up and

leaned against the headboard. Eva looked away and then turned to stare at me.

"I was wondering if you wanted to go and grab some dinner. We've been here all day and the last thing on either of our minds was food. I'm hungry, so I know you're hungry."

How was I supposed to break it to her that I didn't plan on staying the night? It was already eleven at night and I knew I wouldn't get home until after midnight. Eva's facial expression told me that she was already expecting me to spend the night with her.

"Ma, we can grab something to eat and then I can drop you back off here. I gotta head home and deal with some shit that happened earlier."

"Figures," she mumbled.

"Why you being like that?"

"Because you told me we're taking a break, don't call me and then you show up here with a hard dick and I allow you to fuck me. That's not fair to me," she complained.

It wasn't fair and I could see how she felt. When I told her that I was taking a break from our situation, she was pissed. Even when she continued to text and call, I would ignore the shit out of her. I mean, why would I answer the phone? My mind was all wrapped into Golden. Deep in my soul, I knew that me and Eva would never be. Yeah, she had all the qualifications when it came to what I wanted in a woman. I mean, she had almost all of them, but there was still something missing, and I couldn't figure the shit out. Even while trying to figure it out, I was still trying to be with her. Out of nowhere, she did that clingy shit which turned me off altogether. As a man, I knew I wasn't right by coming in her home, fucking her and then bouncing back home. I'm all about admitting when I'm wrong and leading her on and fucking with her feelings was fucked up on my part.

"I'm sorry, Eva. It was fucked up of me to come in here and do you like that, I apologize. Shit had got hard for me, and I came to something familiar, and that shit wasn't fair to you."

"It wasn't. Now what? We go back to acting like we don't know each other? I'm so in love with you, Yoshon. How can I act like I'm not when I am and want to be with you?" she poured her feelings out to me.

I had love for Eva, but I didn't love her. She was someone I cared about and never wanted bad to come onto her, yet I wasn't in love with her. The same feelings she felt for me wasn't reciprocated when it came to her. She was someone that I wanted to fuck when I was in the mood, and occasionally share a meal with. When I thought about a wife, kids, and a life together, Eva wasn't the woman for me.

"Eva, we can't continue to do this same song and dance. I don't want to hurt you, and I can see I've already done that. We can always be friends and I'm here whenever you need me."

"But, you're just not in love with me. It's that assistant, right?"

"Nah, this isn't even about her. This is about me and you, and you continue to bring her into this shit. I've felt like this before you knew she was staying with me."

She climbed out the bed and wrapped her robe around her body. "Yoshon, forget about the food, me and everything that has me tied to it. I'm a fool to believe that we would be more than fuck buddies. For six months, you sat there and got what you wanted out of the deal, and me? All I got was free fucking meals and dick. It doesn't take six months for us to put a title on what we're doing."

Jumping out of bed, I grabbed my pants and pulled them up. "What you failed to realize is that I'm not every fucking body. I'm Yoshon Santana, and I move how I want to move. If it takes six months or sixteen months, that's what the fuck it'll take."

"Just go." Was all she said as she walked into the bathroom and shut the door behind her. I could tell she was hurt and I hated that it had to be me that ended up hurting her.

Pulling on the rest of my clothes, I grabbed my keys and dipped. While she was giving me the out, I was going to take that shit. Knowing Eva, she would come out the bathroom crying and screaming if I stood around. In a few days, I would call and check up on her. Eva was strong and knew how to handle herself. A man that deserved her would come around and sweep her off her feet, and I was sure of it. I just wasn't that man for her. I'd rather be real with her now, then lead her on and hurt her even more. She wasn't the woman for me, and I finally said it loud and clear. After being with Golden, I got that feeling. I couldn't even compare the shit to how I felt with Ashleigh; it was different. It was different, yet it felt good. I wanted to be with her every waking moment. Even while I was pissed with her, I still wanted to go home and hold her in my arms.

Soon as I pulled off, I dialed Grape back and waited for him to answer. When he did, I could tell he was asleep. "Damn, what the fuck you been in? After you left, I been hitting your jack."

"I was at Eva's crib. I'm on my way back to the crib now, what's up?"

"That Fear situation... who the fuck knew he was married to Golden. You think this a set up?" The main reason me and Grape had been friends for years was because he looked at shit from every angle. While I wasn't thinking that way, he was already ahead of the game and ready for whatever I wanted done.

"Nah, you saw how she damn near jumped out her skin when she saw him?"

"True, just needed to see what you thought. Her son was scared as shit too; fuck is that about?"

"I don't know. Check it; I do plan to speak to Fear's ass and find out what the fuck this shit is about."

"All I heard was beat and rape and was ready to lay that nigga down. If it wasn't your crib and Pit Pat wasn't there, I would have."

"We'll let him rock. I'm heading to the crib to shower and get some sleep. Eva's ass got all emotional about us not being together and shit."

"The fuck did you show up there in the first place? You already know how she feel about you, why the fuck confuse shit even more for her?"

"Pussy good, I guess. I was driving and the next thing I know, I pulled up in front of her crib. She's familiar, you know."

"Yeah, familiar means she'll make issues. Golden doesn't tell the truth once, and you're running back to your old fling. Kid, get your shit together, man."

"Shut the fuck," I joked. "It happened once, that's all. I'm 'bout to head to the crib, so I'll holla at you in the morning."

"Bet. One thing... did you speak to your sis?"

"Nah, I haven't heard from her in a minute, she good?"

"I'm just asking... yeah, she good. Go ahead and get home, holla at you tomorrow," he told me and we ended the call.

I didn't like the tone in Grape's voice when he mentioned Yolani. We hadn't spoken in a minute and I knew I needed to pull up on my sister. It didn't take me long to make it back to the crib. When I pulled up, all the lights were out. Knowing Pit Pat, I knew she was in bed, but up waiting until she heard me come through the door. I hit the alarm on my whip and made my way into the crib. Disarming the alarm, I quickly stepped in and set it back again before making my way to my room. As I walked passed Golden's room, I wanted to stop inside and talk. Knowing how angry I was with her for lying, I knew that me going in her room tonight would end with me going the fuck off on her tonight, and I didn't need to wake Gyan up.

I pushed my door opened and walked through the seating area and made it to my bedroom. When I got to my bedroom area, Golden was in my bed reading a book. She was always reading a damn book and would want to discuss it soon as she was finished. I cleared my throat and she looked up from her book. With a weak smile, she placed the book down and stared right into my eyes. My eyes couldn't help to wander up her legs as she laid in my bed in a pair of my boxers and sports bra.

"Hey," she softly greeted me.

"What's good?" I nodded my head as I kicked my boots off and placed my jewelry on the dresser.

She pulled her legs under her and rubbed her hands together. "I'm sorry, Yoshon. I didn't mean to hurt you, I swear," she started.

"Oh yeah? You didn't mean to lie to me?"

"You know I didn't, Yoshon. I had to protect myself; I had to make sure that you knew nothing about my past. Maybe, I wanted to create a different life? Not think about the past year of hell that me and Gyan had been going through. It felt nice having someone not know who I am, or who I'm married to. Yoshon, everything I told you about myself was the truth. I'm the same person; I just lied about my past."

"See, what you don't understand is that you lied. How the fuck am I supposed to trust anything that you have to say out of your mouth? Is Gyan even your child? Or did you kidnap his ass while you were on the run?"

"I need to move, Yoshon. We're going to be leaving in a few days, soon as you deposit my first check."

"The fuck?" Out of everything, I didn't think she would say some shit like this out of her mouth.

"He knows where we are, and I can't risk anything happening to us. Yoshon, I appreciate everything that you and Pit Pat have done for us, but I can't stay here and act like he doesn't know where I lay my head at night."

"Why you so scared of him?"

"You went deaf when I screamed he beat and raped me?"

"Nah, but he did say you tried to kill yourself and your son, so can you see where the fuck the confusion comes in at?"

Sniffling, she looked away and then stared me right in the eyes. "After I had Gyan, I was overwhelmed with everything. I didn't have a mother there to help or teach me how to be a mother, and I didn't have a man there to help me either. Grand was busy with the streets and was never home. Gyan was a fussy baby and cried all day long, so yes, I went through postpartum depression. I could barely pull myself together to get out the bed, so how was I supposed to raise a newborn baby? Grand was in and out, and when I needed his shoulder to cry on, he told me to man up and went on about how his mother raised him and his sister without a man or money, so I needed to be grateful that I had both and stop whimpering around." She looked away and tears dropped from her eyes.

"Don't speak on it if it's too hard." I sat in front of her on the bed.

"No," she sniffled. "I need to get this out. My doctor saw the signs immediately and put me on medicine. The medicine helped for a while until I started to feel suicidal. I would literally hold Gyan while feeding him and thinking of killing the both of us. We didn't have a place or reason to be in this world. One night, I packed Gyan in his carrier and got behind the wheel of my car. I pulled out of our gates doing ninety miles per hour, zipped right by Grand and didn't even know it. He circled back around and followed behind me while calling my cell phone. I ignored him and drove to a drop off I knew about. Thinking back, I get chills because how could I have thought of killing myself and my son?" she cried out and I reached out and held her in my arms.

"I'm sorry, Gold. I didn't know that shit and wished you would have told me sooner." I kissed her on the forehead as she broke down.

She leaned up and wiped her face. "Long story short, Grand was able to get me to slow down. I told him everything, and he got our son out the car and got me the help I needed. It was a side effect of the medicine that caused the suicidal thoughts. I've been on different medicines since and they've all made me feel like death. I wasn't myself and felt like I was just a shell of myself. When Gyan turned a year old, I finally got it together and got rid of my medicine. I started working out, bringing him along with me and doing for myself. I also had Grand's sister who talked me out of most my crazy times."

"Damn, you should have told me ahead of time."

"Yeah, and what would that have solved? You still would have been looking at me differently," she admitted. "Grand isn't who is trying to portray himself to be. He beat the hell out of me in front of Gyan, dragged me upstairs and then raped the hell out of me. He did it right in the middle of our bedroom like I wasn't anything to him, then chuckled and told me to go fix our son something to eat when he was done. Yoshon, I don't expect you to fight my battles, I just want you to understand them."

"You're not leaving."

"I have to," she tried to convince me.

If only she knew how much and how far I would go to protect both she and Gyan. Hearing the shit that nigga put her through pissed me the fuck off. What kind of nigga got a wife and then did the fuck shit he did to her? A woman was to be cherished, praised and protected. In return, you would get loyalty from them. Women were the most easiest creatures on the earth to please. While we thought they wanted the world handed to them on a silver platter, they wanted the most simple shit. Changing the trash or fixing them food was shit that meant the world to them.

"Nah, let me holla at him and see where his head is at." She nodded her head, and I leaned over and covered my lips with hers. She held the side of my face and then I pulled away. "You trust me?"

"Yes," she smiled.

"Golden, you make me feel like I could move the fucking earth with my pinky. On the real, you make me the happiest I've been in a while, and I'm feeling the fuck out of you. Don't lie to me anymore, you hear?"

"I promise," she replied as she allowed me to pull her on my lap and kiss her on the neck. Touching, kissing and smelling her were all senses that let me know that this was what it was supposed to feel like. With Eva, shit felt forced, and half the time I didn't want to do it. With Gold, I wanted to hold onto her and never let her ass go.

"I came from Eva's crib and we fucked." I'm a grown man, and I wasn't about to tiptoe and lie about shit. If I was expecting her to be honest, then I needed to be truthful too.

"I know. I can smell a woman on you. It's fine. I pissed you off, so we're even." She shrugged her shoulders. Taking her face into my hands, I made sure we locked eyes before I spoke.

"What? Nah, I don't give a fuck if you ran over my damn hand, it doesn't give me the right to hurt you back. Don't give no nigga an excuse as to why he could hurt you... hear me?"

"I hear you, Yoshon," she replied and looked away. "Is she going to be a problem? If that's where your heart is, then go and be with her. I never want to stand in the way of something that existed before I came into your life."

"She's never been a problem and she won't be a problem. If she becomes a problem, I promise I'll be the first to let you know."

"Okay," she smiled. "I'm going to sleep with Gyan tonight. I feel like I need to be close to him," she explained.

"Ight bet. Have a good night," I held her face and placed a kiss on her lips. She stared at me for a minute before she hugged me tightly.

"Thank you."

"For what?"

"For listening to me without judgment. You didn't have to, and you could have kicked me out, instead, you listened and believed me after I lied to you."

"Your mouth can lie all day, but your actions told me the truth soon as you laid eyes on him. Get some sleep and we'll talk in the morning."

"Okay." I watched as she grabbed her book and switched out of the room. I hated to see her go but loved watching her leave.

HA

3

Hazel

I DIDN'T KNOW what to do, say or feel. It was one thing to deal with Yolani lying about filing our marriage license. On top of that, I had to worry about being pregnant and Yolani having a damn addiction to the very thing she supplied on the streets. It was something I couldn't even fathom right now. To add the cherry on top, Denim wouldn't stop calling me or stopping by at the shop. Right now, I wasn't ready to sit down and deal with this baby. Did I even want to have this baby? He never stopped to ask me how I felt about being pregnant with his child. Denim was who I was supposed to be with, yes, but did that mean I was meant to have a child with him – this way? I leaned back on the couch and shook my head. Right in front of me were the papers that Denim had given to me. Yolani hadn't made it home last night and I didn't know what I was going to say to her. The look on Pit Pat's face broke me more than the fact that Yolani was on drugs. You could tell she was broken and didn't know what to do.

This was a woman that had a solution for every issue that arose, and she couldn't fix the one issue she knew needed to be fixed asap.

What did I bring up first? Did I even bring up the fact that I was pregnant? The more I thought of everything, the more of a headache came on. I tried to be everything to Yolani, and to hear that she didn't file our certificate hurt me like someone tossed a brick at my head. All she had to do was one thing and she never did it. This entire time she had me believing we were something that we weren't. What was her purpose of this, and if I just found out, who else knew about this? It was all questions that consumed me and made me wonder what the hell was actually going on. Soon as I leaned back in the chair, I heard the door chime and knew it was Yolani. The way she hit the glass on our front door was something she always did when closing the door. My heart felt like it was about to stomp right out of my damn chest and onto the coffee table. Then, my stomach was in knots, and I didn't know what the hell to do or feel? I felt anger with everything that had been revealed to me, but how did I convey that, so it wasn't so damn harsh when it came out my mouth?

"Baby, why you sitting in the damn dark?" She turned the light on in the formal living room. No one ever sat in here, but today, I felt I needed to sit here or else I would use the TV, food or anything else to distract me from bringing up shit that needed to be brought up. She eyed the little box that was under her side of the bed. "Why the fuck you going in my shit?" her tone quickly changed.

"Going through *your* stuff? Last I checked, this was my house too."

"I don't give a fuck about it being your crib. If I have shit that's mine, you don't need to be fucking touching it" She grabbed the box up and started out the room.

"How long?" was all I called out behind her.

"Don't try and sit here and judge me with your judgmental

ass. How the fuck you know I'm using this shit? You didn't even fucking ask before you got to assuming shit," she barked on me, which told me she wasn't only using it, but she was too deep into it.

"Yolani, I'm not a fucking fool. How long have you been using?"

"The fuck you mean how long I've been using? I've been working from home, not fucking doing drugs." She tried to convince herself, because she damn sure wasn't convincing me.

"All that sniffling, the jittery behavior, and the agitation all makes sense now. Why, Yolani?" She had it all. A wife, money and a family that loved the hell out of her. What was her reason for using drugs? She had no damn reason except for her being so damn selfish and only thinking of herself.

"It's fucking winter! The fuck you mean, sniffling means I'm on coke. I'm fucking cold, Hazel!" she screamed and punched the wall with her free hand.

"Take a drug test."

"Fuck you!" she spewed with so much hate. I had to remind myself this wasn't Yolani speaking; this was the drugs. I was trying to take them away from her and she was getting defensive.

"Fuck me? I guess it's easy to say shit like that to your fake wife, huh?" I stood up and tossed the papers in her face. "All these years I sat here like a fool and you never filed those damn papers."

"How the fuck you got these papers? You doing research and shit now? You out here playing fucking Columbo instead of being a damn wife, huh?"

"This isn't about me and you know it. It's about how you've lead me on and lied to me for years all because you wanted to have me to yourself. Sitting here all day, I thought of all the times we've been through, and you wanted me, and you didn't want anybody else to have me. So, you went ahead and proposed and then faked a fucking marriage. You're worse than Love and Hip Hop, Yolani."

"Damn, I got fucking cold feet. I saw the man that vowed to love my moms, sit there and murk her in cold blood. It had me shook and made me backpedal. I love you though, Hazel, that shit don't change."

"Oh please. Yolani, you use that same excuse about your mother for everything. You use it when it benefits your ass only. Whenever I try to talk to you about it, or tell you to seek a thera-pist, you downplay it and act as if you don't think about it anymore. Now, it's convenient for you to use it, right? Take this ring, house and kiss my damn ass." I pulled my ring off my finger and headed upstairs.

Of course, she followed behind me once she realized that I wasn't listening to shit she was saying. I didn't want to hear a damn thing that she had to say. She knew when she mentioned her mother I had a soft spot for her and that would cause me to comfort her. While I spent our entire relationship comforting her ass, where the fuck was she when I needed someone to lean on? She was always in the streets handling something that was more important to her than me.

"You want to sit here and act like your shit all perfect. I dabble in coke occasionally," she admitted.

"There's no fucking dabbling in coke. You either do it or you don't. The fact that you're sitting here trying to downplay how much drugs you actually do is sickening."

"What's sickening is knowing my fucking wife is bouncing up and down on dick when I'm not around, but got my ass sucking her pussy up and down while we're in Miami!" she raised her voice and tossed her little coke box.

My voice was caught in my throat. I just knew my shit was airtight and that I had been careful with Denim. We didn't do anything out in the open, and I went to his apartment, or a hotel when we wanted to get out of his apartment. Knowing Yolani, she probably had someone watching me because she could take that I was so good to her. It made her feel better that she had some dirt to dirty me up some.

"I don't know what you're talking about." I grabbed my suitcase out the closet and went to grab some clothes to toss inside of it.

"Your ex didn't come back into town? You ain't been getting dicked down from him? Since we being real, come be real, thot."

"Take that back!" I screamed and pointed my finger at her. "Don't try to paint a picture that isn't true about me, Yolani. Yes, I got some dick, and I loved it. You know what else I loved? I loved that it wasn't only about the dick, he spent time with me, cherished me and wanted to flaunt me around. Instead, I was too damn foolish and stupid to see that I was hiding a man that would give me the world, for a woman that couldn't even give me her last name."

"Fuck outta here, that soft ass nigga ain't got no heart. You're lucky to be with a nigga like me. Look at this crib, your whips, your account, how the fuck you get all of that? I'm the one that bust my ass to provide that shit to you."

"And if I would have known the price I had to pay was you being a damn crackhead, I would have rejected all of this," I replied and wiped away a tear. I refused to cry about this shit any longer. Yolani showed me that she was for herself and that I either needed to get with the program or get the hell on. I chose to get the hell on, not only for myself, but if I decided to keep my child, I couldn't subject them to her drug-addicted ass.

"The last bitch that called me a crack head didn't live to speak about it."

"You hate what you are. Oh, my bad; you do coke, so you're a damn coke head. Except, coke is a gateway to fucking crack!" I yelled and shoved some more clothes into the suitcase.

While I was busy packing and not paying attention to crackhead Sue, I looked up, and she had a gun pointed right at me. All the air out of my body came out and I stood like a deer in head-lights. Did she just pull a fucking gun on me? She pulled a gun on me like I was some rival gang in the street, instead of the woman that had made her house a damn home.

"If we weren't done before, we're officially done. I just want to thank you. Because of you, I don't have to go through no dumb ass divorce or anything like that. Get some help, Yolani," I said and grabbed my suitcase off the bed.

"Where the fuck you think you're going? One incident and you trying to leave without working shit out." She sat the gun on the dresser.

Although I should have been hauling ass out of that house, I plopped on the bed. I felt like I was being mind-fucked or some-thing. What did she mean one incident and I'm trying to leave? It had been a buildup of shit she had done to me. Never coming home, always too busy to spend time with me and the constant disrespect anytime I decided to bring up my issues. Now, I had to find out that I wasn't legally married, and she had a drug addic-tion; it was time for me to chuck up the deuces and leave well enough alone.

"It's funny that you think it's one incident when it's a plethora of fucking incidents that had pushed me to this moment here. I should have been left and I didn't. Instead, I tried to find the good in you, and as of lately, it hasn't been much. You see, I love you, and I tried to be there for you and you continued to kick me and not want to be the woman you promised me you would be."

"Don't leave. I'll leave," she told me instead. I could tell my words had gotten to her. This whole situation was crazy.

"No, I want to leave. You pulling a gun out on me doesn't make me feel any better or makes me feel safe enough to close my eyes and get some rest."

"Oh, word?"

"Word. You lied to me and you lied to me about something that meant a lot to me. I wanted to be your wife even when my family told me I was a damn fool. Silly of me to think that you would change everything for me. Instead, all you have done was continue to make me look like a damn fool."

She tried to say something else, but me leaving the room stopped her. I pulled my luggage down the stairs and into the back of my car. Who knew what the future held for me? What if I did work things out with Yolani, or me and Denim worked out and welcomed a baby into this world. At this moment, I didn't know where the hell my next step to the road that would lead me into my future was. All I knew was that I didn't feel safe sleeping under the same roof as Yolani. Drugs made you paranoid and you weren't yourself when you took them. The last thing I needed was to be sleep and this bitch trying to stab me to death. As long as she continued to be in denial about having a drug habit, I wasn't going to be anywhere near her.

"You need to come on out of this room. Mo is in the living room waiting for you." My mother held my bedroom door opened.

Tossing and turning in the bed, I leaned up. "I'll be down," I replied and she closed the door behind her.

Coming back home wasn't in my plans at all. I could have stayed with Pit Pat and Yoshon, but that meant more questions I didn't want to answer right now. My parents had a bunch of questions, and I'm sure they were waiting on the perfect moment to dive into them, yet I hadn't given it to them. It had been two days since I arrived on their front steps with a suitcase and Popeyes chicken. Right then and there, my mama wanted to get right into it, and I stopped her. For the last two days, I hadn't picked up my phone or left this room, except to eat or use the bathroom. Even then, I would wait until my parents left to go downstairs to eat. It was funny because I didn't have an appetite at all. Still, I knew I needed to eat for this baby, so it was the main reason I pulled myself out of bed.

Hearing Mo was downstairs wasn't a surprise to me at all. She had been calling me and I hadn't answered. Because it was Mo, my best friend, sister and confidant, I knew the shop was taken care of. I didn't need to tell her what needed to be done, she already knew and handled it. Pulling on a pair of sweats and a shirt, I slipped my feet into some Givenchy slides and headed downstairs. My hair was pulled on top of my head and hadn't been combed in days. Still, I didn't care about any of that shit. All I cared about was getting over this feeling that felt like I was having a heart attack or something. I knew it was my heart hurting because it had just been broken two days prior.

"You look like shit," Mo commented when I came sliding into the living room. She remained seated with her legs crossed.

"Hazel, I'm running to the grocery store before your father gets home. If you need anything, let me know."

"Ma, I'm grown. I don't need you to continue to tell me to call you," I snapped. It was fucked up, and she didn't deserve it, and I knew it.

"If you're not here when I get back, kiss those babies for me, Mo." She cut her eyes at me and headed out the door.

"Now, I know you better apologize when she steps foot back into this house," Mo wasted no time getting in my ass.

"She's been doing that since I came. My mother barely called when I was living with Yolani, so why would I need to call her if I needed her?"

"You're not a mother, so you don't know how she felt. You got married to Yolani and pushed your parents further out of your life. Then, you come and end up on their doorsteps with a suitcase. She's worried about you."

"It's all too much. I would have checked into a hotel, except I knew she would come looking for me there. At least here, I know she wouldn't show up here because of my parents."

"If she loved you the way she said she does, your parents, God or anybody couldn't stop her from getting to you. What's going on?" She touched my hand and the tears flew down my cheeks.

"I'm pregnant with Denim's baby, Yolani is on coke, and then I find out that we're not legally married." Mo snatched her hand back from me and stared at me weird.

"Are you kidding me?" was all she said to me. I wished like hell I was kidding. After explaining everything that went down, she gasped and hugged me tightly. "I'm sorry, Hazel. Before anything else, what are you going to do about the baby?"

"I don't know, Mo. I really don't know what the hell I'm going to do; I'm so scared. A kid is something that I've always said I wanted, but now that it's here, I don't know what to do with myself."

"That baby is a blessing. Whatever you decide, you know I'll support you, but don't let the situation waver your feelings about becoming a mother."

"Mo, I don't know anymore. I've tried and tried, but I think me and Yolani are done. Drugs, Mo? Drugs?"

"I wish I could tell you that I didn't see this coming, but I did. Yolani thinks of herself and she has ever since you guys were friends. Why do you think I never wanted to hang around with y'all? Yolani is selfish."

"Why didn't you say anything? You allowed me to marry her and play house with her, all while you and my parents knew she was selfish and hated her."

"Baby, I don't hate a damn person... we voiced our opinion, and you told us what you wanted to do. What did you expect us to do? Lock you in your bedroom? You're a big girl and needed to do what you need to do."

"Well, look at where it has gotten me now?"

"And that's not me or your mama's fault; it's your own. You stood by and stuck around when clearly she didn't deserve you. That's a decision you decided to make."

"Mo, what am I going to do?"

"That's up to you, baby girl. You need to follow your heart. I know you love Yolani, but are you prepared to be second when it comes to her? With Denim, you know he wants to be with you, are you prepared to be his everything, because that man loves the hell out of you."

"This is all too much." I leaned back on the couch and put my head back. All of this was coming at me too fast and all at the same time. Usually, things happened to people and you gave them time to think about stuff, but I had three very real situations staring me right back in the face.

"I know it is. Have you spoke to Denim about the baby?"

"Yeah, and he wants me to keep it. Mo, he wants us, the baby and to be together and he has said it multiple times, and I've ignored him."

"You have what you've been wanting from Yolani with Denim, and you're ignoring him?"

"He's not Yolani though," I sighed. "I love Denim, I do. Part of me feels like if I move on with him, I'm leaving Yolani. She lost her mother and father; I don't want her to lose me too."

"Girl, stop. Yolani's mother died when she was twelve years old. I'm not saying there's a time limit on mourning, especially when the murder happened right before her eyes, but she's twenty-seven making the same ass excuses she did when she was twelve. She hasn't went to get help or a damn thing, so you need to stop using that excuse and allowing her to use the same excuse."

I couldn't do anything except laugh because I had just said the same thing to Yolani two days before. Why was it that she couldn't use that excuse, but I was able to use that same excuse?

"Look, I need to get Jahryan to his coding classes." She stood up and grabbed her keys.

"Coding? I swear you're raising some black magic children."

"Yep, his school offers it at a college near the house. If I don't do anything else, I gotta make sure my kids are straight."

"Indeed. Kiss them for me and tell them auntie will see them soon. How's the salon?"

"The salon is good. I had an issue with another technician, but she was straightened out soon as I told her could leave early, and I'll refer all her clients to other techs in the shop."

"Those girls are scared of your ass," I joked. It was true, but Mo hated when I said that half the shop feared her ass.

"Uh huh. Let me go pick up my baby, and I'll see you later. And you better apologize to your mama," she scolded.

"I will!" I yelled out as she closed the door behind her. At last, I was able to lay down and have some thoughts to myself. The thoughts soon took the back seat because I was finally able to close my eyes and get some sleep.

4

Yolani

"YOU MEAN to tell me that this nigga showed up to the city?" I spoke to Grape as we sat in one of the traps. It had been a little over a week since I had seen or spoken to Hazel. Part of me was worried about her, then the other part of me said fuck her. When shit got rough, she was the first to dip instead of trying to work the shit out. Yeah, I lied about being married and I admit it was my fault and fears that stopped me from filing the correct papers. Me and Hazel were jumping right into this shit full fledge. While she was excited and planning the rest of our lives together, I was thinking about my money, my crib and my freedom being tossed out the window. I told myself I would file it a month after we got married and never got around to it. Shit, I didn't think she would ever find out and now that she knew, I could see the hurt across her face. If she didn't trust me before, I knew damn well she wasn't about to trust my ass anymore.

"Yeah, and he said he been hitting you back, and he ain't

heard shit from you." Grape started to get on my case, like he usually did.

"I mean, he did hit me up, and I admit that, but I had other shit going on too."

"Like?" He waited for an explanation and I didn't have one. Well, I did, but I couldn't tell him that I almost beat the life out of Cherry because she called me a crackhead, or that I had a fraud marriage on my hands.

"Nigga, my shit personal. I don't see you over there trying to tell me about your fine ass sister in medical school."

Grape was protective of his baby sister. They both grew up in the same hood me and Yoshon did, except Grape got her out. Soon as she graduated high school, she went on to college and then medical school. When she came home from school, he would go ghost and spend all his time with her. I was a bad influence and he didn't want her around me. As fine and smart as his sister was, she needed to be around a nigga like me. Shorty was about to be a doctor and I could be getting the legal drugs on the streets. There's ways I could go about getting them, but if I had a connect to get the drugs that would be even better.

"Leave Gianna alone," he sternly warned. "Especially bringing her up in here." He got upset.

It was then I looked around and noticed the damn trap was empty. Usually, I would have caught onto the shit when I first walked in, but today, there wasn't nobody in here, and the shit looked empty as fuck. Grape noticed that I was observing my surroundings and cleared his throat but didn't say anything.

"Where the fuck is everybody?"

"Working," he nonchalantly replied.

"Working? This is one of the busiest trap houses, what the fuck you mean they working?"

"Your brother had the traps moved." He finally stopped beating around the bush and told me what I had already confirmed with his nonchalant attitude and empty trap house.

"What the fuck for?"

"You already know you need to take that shit up with him. I don't get involved in y'all shit, and you know that."

"For someone who doesn't get involved, you seem to know every fucking thing that happens before I do."

"You already know why I know. That shit don't mean I'm involved in y'all shit."

Rolling my eyes. "Yeah, what the fuck ever."

"Go talk to your brother." Was what he said and all he ever said.

Anytime I came to his ass; he always sent me back to my brother. If I wanted to talk to Yoshon's big headed ass, I would have. Except, I knew my brother and all he wanted to do was try to get me to slow down on working and be in touch with my feelings. This nigga was more emotional than I was. Just because he wore his heart on his sleeve didn't mean he wouldn't murk a nigga at the drop of a dime. Yoshon used to be more ruthless before Ashleigh passed. It was like that nigga's ruthless soul left his body when she was buried into the ground.

"Yeah, what the fuck ever!" I barked and stood up from the table in the house. It was the only piece of furniture in that bitch and I was just noticing that.

Grape never called behind me or try to calm me down. He truly didn't give a fuck about the situation and I never expected him to. "Yo," he called behind me.

Shocked, he called behind me, I turned around curious as to what he had to say. "Big Ben is getting out next week."

"How the fuck that happened?" My heart was beating fast as fuck.

"Technicality," he responded.

Turning around, I walked out the trap and didn't bother to say a damn thing. Big Ben was someone that I respected more than anyone, except my brother. Big Ben was my first love and the first man who took my virginity. If I didn't like women, Big Ben would have been the nigga I ended up with. We were friends before anything and been through a bunch of shit together. My family didn't even know I had gotten pregnant, had a son and gave him up for adoption to Big Ben's oldest sister. If I knew I was pregnant, I would have gotten an abortion instead of going through the pain of having a damn baby. The way I found out was crazy as fuck. I was admitted to the hospital for the flu and found out I was six months pregnant. I wasn't even showing or had no kind of fucking clue that I was pregnant with a baby. Big Ben wanted to be a family and raise this baby, and I had other plans.

Women were what I was interested in and wanted to be with. The only man that ever turned me on was Big Ben. I didn't even think he turned me on; it was more our friendship and his loyalty that did that. I didn't want no damn kids and I damn sure wasn't about to be someone's baby mama. Yoshon was showing me the ropes to the business and I couldn't come with him talking about I was pregnant. Not to mention, it was when I transitioned to wearing men's clothing and getting tattooed up. The fuck I look like being pregnant. For the remainder of my pregnancy, I hid out in my apartment and chilled the fuck out. When it was time for me to have the baby, my ass went to Staten Island, had the baby and signed the papers over to Big Ben's sister. I cried for a few weeks because I didn't think that this shit would be emotional for me. I thought it would be like a damn drug deal.

The fucked-up part was that Big Ben got knocked soon after, so we never got to deal with the shit. After the hospital, I didn't want to talk to anybody. I cut my family out, and Big Ben was just a reminder of the son that resembled him. His sister took over raising our son and now he was ten years old now. The crazy shit was that he lived three blocks down from one of the trap houses. Big Ben's sister kept me informed and I made sure she always had some money. The little nigga ran past me one day and I had to go in the bathroom at my trap and shed a tear or four. He looked just like me and Big Ben; the shit was crazy.

Hearing that Big Ben was coming home meant I was going to be forced to deal with all the skeletons that I had buried. He was never a fan of giving his seed up to his sister. His hands were tied because he couldn't raise a child alone. How the fuck was he going to run the streets, and take care of a child? It wasn't part of my plan and I damn sure wasn't about to be raising a child I knew I didn't want. My mouth said one thing and then my heart said another. It pained me to know I had a son out there and he knew nothing about me. I made Big Ben's sister promise that she would never tell him. He looked nothing like her, and everything like his supposed uncle, which was really his father. I knew one thing, and that was that I needed to avoid Big Ben's ass like the fucking plague.

5

Yoshon

"WHAT'S GOOD, FAMILY?" I greeted everyone as I came into the kitchen. Pit Pat was sitting for once at the table with Gyan while Golden prepared breakfast. She held out a mug of coffee and pointed to the empty seat next to Gyan. "Thank you." I grabbed the cup and made my way over to the table.

Golden maneuvered around the kitchen with ease while Pit Pat sat with the newspaper and a mug filled with peppermint tea. "How did you sleep last night?" Golden broke her silence.

Since our talk the other day, we both had been focusing on work and not so much on each other. When I walked by her bedroom at night, it took everything in me not to go in there, pin her against the wall and suck on her lips for the rest of the night. Since shit had been about business, I kept it about business and didn't blur the lines until she was ready to.

"I tossed and turned for a bit, got a little sleep. You?"

"I was up reading most of the night. Don't get too much sleep these days." She flipped a pancake onto a plate and brought it to Pit Pat.

The reason she didn't sleep was because she was constantly worried about Grand. I watched how she checked all the locks when it was time for bed, or how she didn't take the same way to Gyan's school in the morning. Seeing her worried like this had me pissed that a nigga had all this power over her. It was the main reason I had agreed to meet up with Grand today to talk. I wanted to hear his side and see what the fuck he had to say. Golden placed everyone's food in front of them and then sat down with a breakfast cereal bar for her meal.

"That's all you gonna eat? With all that ass and body, your ass ain't eating no damn cereal bar," I joked and she rolled her eyes at me with a smirk.

"Mom has a big booty. She told me she got it from her mama," Gyan repeated something his mother had told him. Pit Pat shook her head and laughed.

"Lil boy, didn't we say what you need to stop repeating?"

"Yes, Pit Pat," he nodded his head.

"Finish up your breakfast and then get washed up for school. And you better ace that math test because we went over it last night a million times," Pit Pat told Gyan.

The way Gyan took to Pit Pat, I could tell he needed someone in his life like this besides Golden. Golden was always the person to discipline him and make sure that he was doing what he should have, but Pit Pat had given her a break and took over with Gyan, and Golden didn't mind. Shit, Gyan didn't even mind because he ate up everything my grandmother taught him.

"Yes, ma'am." He shoved some pancakes into his mouth and continued to eat until he finished his food.

When Pit Pat finished, she looked over at Golden. "Look at the bags under your eyes, chile. Why aren't you getting any sleep? You're safe here; you don't need to worry about that man any longer."

"Y'all just don't understand," she shook her head and bit into her cereal bar. "He has hurt me and he will do it again. Somebody won't let me leave." She cut her eyes at me.

"You said you trusted me, right?" I asked her calmly. She rolled her eyes and went to finish her cereal bar like I hadn't asked her a question. "You heard me, Golden."

"I do trust you, Yoshon. Listen, I don't want to talk about this shit right now," she snapped and got up from the table.

Gyan watched his mama leave the table and continued to eat. Pit Pat turned her attention to me. "I thought I told the both of you to fix this?"

"We did. Don't worry about it. I want to know what's going on with you?" Shit with Pit Pat hadn't been the same since she returned from Yolani's crib. She was quiet, kept to herself and I could tell she wasn't telling me something.

"I'm old. Change in my mood and attitude comes with the territory." She tried to bypass what I was asking her.

"Pit, I know you more than I know myself."

"Boy, I know me more than I know anybody else. I've been with myself since I came busting out my mama's love below," she chuckled. "I am fine, okay." She stood up and grabbed both her and Gyan's empty plates.

"When you're ready, will you tell me?" Knowing my grandmother, she wouldn't tell me. She was the type of woman that handled things herself and barely boggled us down with her issues.

"Soon as I have some issues, I'll be the first to bring it to you, Yosho," she called me the childhood nickname that she had given me.

"Gyan, let's get up and get your backpack," she told Gyan and he jumped up to go do what she said. "You go talk to Golden, that's the only woman you should be concerned about right now," she told me.

It didn't make sense for me to go and speak to Golden right

now. The person that she was so scared of was living in the next state over, and she was worried. Grand raped and beat her like she wasn't nothing and she was scared of that happening again. I wished she knew that I would protect the shit out of her and he would never get close to her again. After I finished my pancakes, I grabbed my keys and headed out. Grand wanted me to meet him at his rental in the city. Part of me just wanted to put the word in and kill this nigga myself, then the other half of me wanted to just hear what the fuck he had to say. I believed everything Golden told me, but it wouldn't have been fair if I didn't listen to both sides before I started laying bodies down.

I pulled up to a luxury building in the Queens and had the valet park my whip for me. The doorman held the door open for me, and I made my way up to the apartment number that he had sent me to. There was a bunch of shit I would have rather been doing today than going to have a conversation with this nigga. To make matters worse, my sister was fucking avoiding the shit out of me. When I called, she dubbed my calls and sent me some bullshit text message. I had something for her ass, and she would find out tonight when she thought she would be in the streets all night. I moved all the trap houses and told everybody to ignore her calls and tell her nothing. While Yolani liked to believe she was a bully in the streets, every once in a while, I had to remind her who the fuck was the real bully in the streets.

Knocking on the mahogany door with the brass trim, I waited until I heard the locks being unlocked. A woman with light skin, brown short bob and glasses opened the door. She smiled and stared at me waiting for me to speak.

"Grand here?"

"Yes, come in," she smiled and held the door open wider for me. Upon walking in, I could this was a woman's crib. She had buddha heads strategically placed all over the crib and the apartment was painted in light hues of lavender. "He's in the living room," she told me and disappeared down the hall.

When I made it into the living room, Grand was sitting with his feet kicked up with a cigarette placed between his fingers. The balcony doors were ajar, and he was too into the video game he was playing to know I had entered the living room.

"You still out here playing boy games, huh?"

"The fuck is that supposed to mean?" he chuckled and put his controller on the coffee table. "What's good, man? I've been hitting your sister up and still haven't heard shit."

"You and me both. I mean, I'm sure she got some shit she got going on right now," I told him. The fuck he wanted me to do about it? The rule me and Yolani had was that we didn't mix business with our own clients. I had my clients, and she had hers, so I wasn't about to make this nigga a fucking client because Yolani couldn't handle her shit.

"Fuck all the personal; this is business." He put his cigarette out and then lit another one right after the other one. Who the fuck knew this nigga was a damn chain smoker?

I knew Grand and we went way back before he started calling himself fucking Fear. He kept in contact with Grape more than he did with me. When Ashleigh died, I stopped fucking with a lot of people and didn't give a fuck anybody. If it wasn't my family or Grape, I didn't fuck with you.

"Yeah, so take that business out on Yolani, not me. I'm here because of the shit that happened at my crib a week ago. The fuck is up with that?"

He pulled on his cigarette and then stared at me through squinted eyes. "You came here for that? Nigga, what's between me and my wife is between me and my wife, why you so concerned?"

"You came in my fucking crib and decided to air dirty laundry out. I think I got every fucking right to come and hear what the fuck is going with the woman staying in my crib."

He let his guard down when I released those words. To him, that meant I wasn't on Golden's side, which I was. The way I worded shit I made him feel at ease, easy enough to talk to me without feeling judged.

"That bi... woman is a fucking lying lunatic. She's lucky I don't go and get her murdered. Lying about me raping and beating on her. You know what the fuck that did to my reputation? My own family looked at me sideways after I was convicted on that shit. Know what's worse, she dipped and left town without even fucking coming to telling me. She's my fucking wife and just dipped after accusing me of some shit like that."

"The way she stared at you and shook, that shit don't seem like she was lying on you. My nigga, I've been around liars my entire life, but shorty couldn't fake that shit. She was damn near about to shake out her damn skin."

"Golden is a fucking actress. She's always been one and good with her emotions, actions, and words. Since she left her mother's crib, she been trying to find a nigga with money. You know how many niggas she went through in Virginia until she landed me?"

"Grandmother?"

"Huh?"

"Since she left her grandmother's crib. She doesn't have a relationship with her mother."

"Yeah, that evil ass bitch." He sat there silently pulling on his cigarette. I could see the guilt all over his face as he reminisced about the shit he did to Golden. "Yoshon, I got the utmost respect for you, but this here isn't your place."

"See, if you had any respect for me, then you would know not to fuck with anything that's mine. You're right, I don't know what y'all got going on, but I know what's going on now and that shit ain't gonna happen under my watch."

"Baby, we have to get ready to go meet my aunt and uncle. You promised you would meet them the next time you came into town, so I arranged dinner at their home."

"Babe, I got you. Let me finish up here and we'll get ready to go."

"Okay," she agreed and floated out the room. This chick had to be some young, dumb bitch attracted to this nigga because of the money.

"Look, what me and my wife got going on isn't your business. We're legally married so if I need to reach out to my wife and handle this situation, then this is what the fuck I'm gonna do. She dipped after getting me arrested; she fucking owes me an apology or something. I could have had her fucking killed for the shit she did to me."

"You didn't." I stood up. "The thing about doing fucked up shit is guilt. My nigga, that guilt eating the shit out of you. I can see the shit all in your face. I'm in retirement, Fear, don't pull me out and make me show you what real fear is," I told him and headed toward the entrance of the living room.

"Yeah ight." He nodded his head and put out his cigarette.

As I turned around, I turned back around and stared at him closing the pack of cigarettes back. "You mentioned everything except your son."

"That bitch took him and ran. That lil' nigga hates me because of his mother's words."

"Or maybe it's his father's actions. Leave Golden and Gyan alone. Anything you need from her, ask me, nigga. Tread lightly, Fear," I chuckled and left the apartment. This nigga had me fucked up if he thought I was going to sit back and act like my Golden wasn't my business.

I hopped in my whip and dialed Golden's number. She answered after a few rings which pissed my ass off. "Why it take you so long to answer the phone?"

"Because I was getting some sleep, Yoshon. Pit Pat has me locked in the room taking a damn nap like a child."

"Don't blame her; you need to fucking sleep. Anyway, put something on tonight because I'm taking you out."

"Taking me where? I'm not leaving Gyan alone," she protested immediately.

"I'll have Grape come to the crib while we're good. Gyan will be straight."

She sighed. "Fine. What should I wear?"

"We're going somewhere laid back. I'm not into nothing fancy. Eva always made me do shit like that."

"Oh, so I'm not good enough for fancy restaurants, but Eva is?"

"Sto—"

"I'm joking. I'll be ready," she giggled.

"Bet. I have a few more things to handle, and then I'm gonna swing by to come and scoop you."

"Bet."

"Why you trying to be like me and shit?"

"Oh please. See you later," she ended the call.

I had to stop at the traps to make sure shit was running smooth. Yolani wasn't handling it because she didn't know where the fuck they were, I needed to make sure they were running smoothly. After, I planned on heading home to change and then go out to dinner with Golden. I needed her to understand that I had her and she didn't need to worry about Grand. The easiest thing would have been to kill that nigga, but if he took his ass back to Virginia, that would be in his best interest.

"WHERE ARE WE GOING? You're wearing sweatpants and shit like we're not about to go out to have dinner or something."

"Don't worry about any of that. We're gonna be good; I don't know why you're all dressed up and shit."

"I'm wearing a dress and a pair of Uggs; I wouldn't classify that as being dressed up." She pulled at her dress a bit before turning her attention out the door.

"I like that."

"What?"

"Seeing your smile. Feels like I haven't seen you smile in a minute."

"Because I haven't."

"I want to see more of that smile. Shit makes me want to smile throughout my day. Promise me you gonna smile more."

"I can't make any pr—" her sentence got cut off by the sound of my phone. When I looked at the number, I immediately answered.

"Em, you good?"

"Hey Yoshon! I'm good. I was just making sure my doctor's office called and told you about the appointment next week."

"Yeah, I'm booking my flight tonight. I have business I need to tend to there, so it'll be a business trip too."

"Cool beans. See you soon," she cheerfully responded and ended the call.

With all the shit I had going on in my life, I somehow lost touch with one of the most important things I had going on. Once meeting Golden, I got so wrapped into her life that my shit was pushed to the back. I didn't blame her because this shit was all on me. Ashleigh was my entire world and there wasn't anything that I wouldn't do for her. We both wanted children and we started the process soon as we got engaged. After trying for a while, we decided to go the IVF route and had some eggs removed and froze. We found one of the best doctors in the country in Los Angeles and decided to work with him. A month after freezing her eggs, she found out that she had ovarian cancer. My baby fought and she fought hard as shit. When she passed, the shit was hard for me. I pushed my family away and didn't speak to people because I was hurting on the inside. A nigga was angry with Ashleigh because she left me.

Almost a year ago, I got a call about Ashleigh's eggs. They asked me about them and what I wanted to do with them? We had a total of two of them just sitting there, ready. I missed my girl so bad that even having a small piece of her I wanted, nah I needed it. I went ahead and hired a surrogate agency and they found me, Emily. She was currently Eight months pregnant with my daughter. Pit Pat, Hazel, Grape or Yolani knew nothing about it. When I made my trips to the west coast, they thought I was there to handle business with the dispensary I had opening there. Yeah, part of that was true, but I was also there to check on the progress with my daughter. Em miscarried our first egg, and this was the last one, so I made sure she had the best care and didn't have to lift a finger. Her days were filled with shopping, yoga, and shit that didn't stress her the fuck out. I wanted to make sure she carried my daughter with no fucking stress, and so far, it had been working in our favor. My daughter was healthy and ready to enter this world in two months.

"You zoned out after that phone call. Are you alright? You're always trying to make sure that I'm good, but who checks up on you besides Pit Pat?"

"Nah, I'm good. Just something I should have been talked to you about."

"Okay, what about?"

"Not here," I quickly replied.

We pulled up to one of my favorite diners out in Crown Heights. It was owned by one of my nigga's, Thor. He opened this shit up a little while back and it had the best food in all of New York. It was a low-key spot, and I wanted to take Golden here to experience some of the food. Plus, I had a taste for the country fried steak that they made with a side of mashed potatoes and corn on the cob. When we walked in, one of the owners, Maggie, greeted me with a warm smile and side hug.

"Haven't seen you around here in a while. Who is your friend?" she smiled as she stood there with her hands in her apron.

"Her name is Golden. You already know what to hook me up

with but give her a minute to figure out what she wants on the menu."

"Alright now... grab a table and someone will come take your order for drinks." She winked and headed behind the bar.

This place was right across the street from the hood, but once you stepped inside, you didn't feel like you were right across from the hood. Whenever I needed a break from Pit Pat and something good, I came here to kick it and watch the game. It was a low-key spot; still, in the same breath, it got a lot of business.

"Yum, everything sounds amazing on this menu, how will I choose?" Golden licked her lips as she stared at the menu.

"Get whatever you want. We can bring leftovers back to the crib."

"As if your grandmother would allow that. Her kitchen doesn't have outside food, and you know that," she giggled.

The waitress came over and took our order while sending over complimentary drinks that Maggie sent over to us. Nodding to her, I sipped the drink and stared back at Golden. She was enjoying her drink and staring at the flat-screen TV.

"You're so fucking beautiful." I gazed into her eyes. She blushed and then looked down at the table. It was something she did whenever I complimented her. The shit drove me crazy because she was beautiful and didn't feel like she had to look down whenever I complimented her. When I told her she was beautiful, I wanted shorty to be smiling so hard that I saw all her damn teeth in her mouth. It spoke volumes to the abuse she said she went through being married to Grand's ass.

"Thank you." She smiled bashfully. "How was your day?"

"I went and spoke to Grand." When his name left my mouth, she looked alarmed and unknowingly gripped the side of the table with her left hand.

"W...why? You didn't need to do that, Yoshon," she raised her voice slightly.

"I know I didn't have to do shit. I went because I fucking

wanted to. My girl telling me a nigga did something to her, so I'm gonna go and check that shit out for myself."

"Wait, you called me your girl?" a slight smile came across her face. "When did that happen?"

"When I slid in between those thighs on Valentine's day. I told you that I got you and I meant that shit. Just because you pissed me off, doesn't mean that I'm done with you. Shit been rough these past few days, but we're gonna work on it."

"It's been rough because I feel like Grand is going to pop out of nowhere. I'm so confused, scared and worried. I can't sleep because I know he has people who can hurt me, and he'll act like it wasn't him. You don't know this man the way I do, and he's fucking wicked." She started to panic and looked around.

I understood how she was scared and how this nigga had a mental and physical hold on her, but she had to know that I wasn't him and I wasn't about to let him lay a hand on her or Gyan. Long as she was under my roof, I was going to protect her with everything I had. She grew quiet, and we both stared at each other as I caressed her hands. This woman was fucking every-thing. Not only was she fine as fuck, but she was smart, a good mother and respectful. I could tell she wasn't one of those chicks who was out there living foul and crazy like Grand tried to portray.

"I gotta tell you something." It was now or never. I could continue to lie to her and my family, or I could be honest and tell them what I had been hiding for the past few months.

"Oh lord, what now? I knew you were too good to be true," she pulled her hands away from mine gently. "What do you have to tell me, Yoshon?" she stared right into my face with concern.

"I'm gonna have a daughter in two months."

"With Eva?" she choked out and held her hand over her chest. Shorty looked as if she was about to have a panic attack in a few.

"Nah," I grabbed her hand back. She listened as I explained everything to her and I couldn't make out her face. I wasn't sure how she was feeling about everything I just laid out to her. She didn't remove her hands from mine or look away. In fact, she stared right into my eyes.

"You wanted a child that bad?"

"I just lost my fiancée. Not only did I lose her, I lost everything we had planned to do together. Marriage, babies and all that shit. Yo, I really felt like a piece of me died at one point. When I got the call, I just wanted a piece of her... feel me?"

"Kids are amazing. I do want you to experience that for yourself, but a surrogate?"

"What's done is done already. I'm thirty-eight about to turn thirty-nine in two months. I want kids, a woman, and all that shit. It can't be with Ashleigh, and I've gotten over the fact that the shit me and her planned will never be, but I can raise our daughter to know her mother and what kind of woman she was."

She removed her hands gently from mine and held the side of the table. "Yoshon, the short time I've known you, I can tell you do for everyone else except yourself, and if this is something you feel in your spirit that you want, who am I to tell you that you're wrong?"

"Appreciate you, Golden." I winked at her.

"This baby is going to change your life, and I don't think you should be focused on a relationship. Neither of us should be focused on a relationship," she corrected herself.

"Wow. Where did that come from?"

"Every baby means something and is precious, but your daughter will mean that much more. She will remind you of her deceased mother. I'm not sure if I'm ready to live in the shadows of another woman."

I understood where she was coming from. Yashleigh was going to know everything about her mother, and I wasn't going to leave shit out about her. She would know that her mother fought hard to be here and eventually God needed her that much more. With Golden, I understood that she would have to live with that fact that I would always talk or bring up my ex-fiancée while trying to build something new with her.

"I understand."

She reached her hand out and touched mine. "In no way am I saying I'm jealous or childish. You should speak about your child's mother, and she should know about the great woman I'm sure her mother was. I'm just..." she paused. "I've been coming second for a long time in my marriage, and I don't want to become second in a relationship too."

"I'm not understanding. You want me to put you before my seed?"

She laughed. "No, Gyan comes before any and every one. What I'm saying is that babies are a lot, and not to mention this circumstance is very different, Yoshon. I don't think you're understanding how much work a baby is. I'll automatically come second when it comes to your fiancée."

"She's dead, Gold. The fuck you getting at?" I was growing irritated because I wasn't understanding what the fuck she was saying to me.

I understood children were a lot. It wasn't like I was expecting Yashleigh to come out the womb walking, talking and changing her own diapers. It also didn't mean that I wouldn't have time to put in to a relationship with Golden. I felt like shorty wasn't being fair with me right about now.

"You just don't understand," she sighed and removed her hair out of her face. "It makes sense to me."

"Nah, the shit sound selfish as fuck to me. I accepted you and not only you, but your son. I don't know where I come in order in your life, but I'm cool just knowing I'm on the list. Gyan means more to you than anything, and he'll always come first when it comes to me and him, which he should. All I want is the same respect for Yashleigh."

"Yashleigh? How did you come up with that?" She tried to

switch the conversation. Golden was good at deflecting when she didn't want to deal with something.

"It's my first letter and her mother's name... You hear what I said?"

"I hear you, Yoshon. I'm your friend always. If you need help with anything, you know that I'm always going to be here for you."

"Yo, what the fuck? You 'bout to have me flip a fucking table in this bitch," I threatened. The shit she was pulling was pissing me off. The things I wanted to do to her wasn't what friends did. For the first time in a while, I actually saw myself building something with a woman other than Ashleigh. In some weird ass way, I felt like Ashleigh sent Golden to me.

When she was on her deathbed, she was more concerned about me being alone. This woman was hours away from dying and was worried about me being alone. That was just how Ashleigh was. She worried and did for everybody before herself. It was something we had in common. We were everything to everyone else, so when we connected, we were everything for each other.

"Calm down. Don't ruin our dinner, please," she calmly stated. "I want to be able to express how I feel without feeling like I'm wrong. It was something I went through with Grand; I promised myself I would never go through it again."

"Fuck it," was all I said. "We have to leave out to Los Angeles for work. You feel comfortable enough for Gyan to stay with Pit Pat?"

"Not with Grand around," she replied back almost instantly.

"If I hired security at the crib and to take him to school?"

"Grand is powe—"

"Don't tell me how powerful a nigga is who relays on me to keep his business going. I'm fucking powerful and if I get my best men to make sure your son is straight, he'll be straight."

"Okay, but do I really need to be there?"

"Yeah," it was all I said for now.

She had to be there because I needed her to do the running around. Before I hired her, I was the one doing the running around for shit. Now that she was my assistant, I was going to make sure she earned her living. Yeah, I wanted to be with her, and I daydreamed about fucking her all over again, but when it came to business, I expected her to conduct it and leave all personal feelings out.

"Okay, fine. I'll be ready to go," she told me.

The food came and we ate in silence. There was so much that I wanted to say and that I planned on saying, but right now wasn't the right time. Golden was in her feelings and I could tell from her actions. Tonight, may have not been the right time to tell her about the daughter I had on the way, but I'd rather her know now then find out from someone else. I didn't regret my daughter, and if I had to choose between Yashleigh and Golden, my daughter would win every time. With me telling Golden, I knew I had to sit down and have a talk with Pit Pat because I had kept it from everyone.

6

Golden

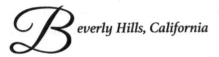everly Hills, California

THINGS with me and Yoshon were weird since our conversation at the diner. I didn't know what to say or do when I was around him. We were cordial and joked on the flight to California. I was always a nervous wreck on planes, and he was really good at keeping me calm. We flew first class and I had champagne to keep me tickled through the entire flight. That was yesterday, and here I was sitting in the Gucci store on Rodeo drive. I should have been going to pick up these documents that Yoshon needed me to pick up from his lawyer's office, or I could have been getting him some food like he requested me to do an hour ago, but I was here staring at this purse. It was so beautiful that I just wanted to walk right out the store with it on my arm.

"I see that you have had your eye on this for quite some time," the sales associate made her way over to me. She had been watching me admire the bag since I first floated into the store.

My plan wasn't to be in the Gucci store to shop for myself. Yoshon forgot his black Gucci belt at home, so of course, he sent me with his card to go and pick one up. Upon walking in, in my mind, I knew which section I needed to head to, but instead, I floated over to the purses, and my feet haven't moved since. It was a black velvet shoulder bag that had Loved on the front of the purse. I was loved, wasn't I? This bag was speaking to me so hard right this minute. Since leaving Virginia, I gave up every single piece of designer gear I had, and I was fine with that. Our lives were way more important than anything I had in my closet.

"I have. This bag is so beautiful."

"Well, don't just stare at it," she giggled and unlocked it from the shelf. "Try it on." She handed me the bag.

I placed it on my arm and moved from side to side, admiring how it looked on me. Even with a pair of sweats, T-shirt and sneakers, this bag made me look like I was about to rip the runway for Nike or Puma.

"I love this bag," I smiled so hard.

"You need to treat yourself and this bag is perfect for that. It'll look perfect with a quick run to the mall or a night on the town with your man." She continued to sell this purse more and more to me.

"You're right. I should." I smiled. "I'll take this and a black men's Gucci belt," I told her.

She smiled hard because her persuading had finally paid off and she was about to receive a huge commission check. I knew I was going to have to apologize to Yoshon for using his black card. I prayed he didn't make me take it back or take money out of my check. At first, I thought me being his assistant was something for play. When he had me filling out papers for taxes, health insurance, etc, I knew he was the real deal. The man owned a lot of businesses and he had them all in order. When he mentioned that Grand had to go through him to provide for his empire, it told me what I had been suspecting all along. He was in the streets and getting legal tender at the same time.

"How will you be paying?" she smiled from behind the counter. Pulling out the card, I gripped it as she snatched it from my fingers.

I watched as she swiped the card, pressed some buttons and then handed me a fancy ballpoint pen to sign the receipt. I expected her to ask for ID or something in that matter, but she didn't. She bagged the purse and belt box up and then came around the counter.

"Thank you for shopping with us today. I placed my card inside the receipt folder in case you ever need to contact me to put something on hold for you." She smiled and handed me my shopping bag once I got to the front door.

"Thank you so much. I appreciate your help today."

With the bags in my hand, I got into the Uber I had ordered and headed back to the Beverly Hills Hotel. This was a hotel I've seen in movies or those reality shows centered around Beverly Hills, and now I was staying in a suite sharing an adjourning patio with Yoshon. My eyes didn't want to see how much he was paying a month on this hotel. There were two bedrooms, and I stayed in one while Yoshon stayed in the other. It was hard not to sneak and get into his bed during the night. Last night, I literally paced the floor fighting with myself. If I wanted to push friendship on him, then I needed to act like a friend. How could I tell him that we were friends while pushing my pussy up on him?

When Yoshon mentioned he had a baby on the way, my stomach dropped. I knew he seemed too good to be true. Especially because he wanted me. God never looked out for me like that, so I waited until the other shoe to drop, and it finally did. This man was about to be someone's father in a month, give or take. It wasn't that I had an issue with him being a father because I was a mother. The difference was that Gyan wasn't a newborn baby. I knew how to take care of him. Yoshon didn't know one thing about raising a baby, let alone a baby girl at that. Pit Pat would, of course, help him with his child, and I would too. However, I couldn't help to think that I would always become second or third in his life. With him sharing a baby with his ex-fiancée, I felt I would always be the third woman in his life. Yoshon wasn't over losing his fiancée and having a daughter with the same DNA as her wasn't going to make it any better. I would be forever coming in last when it came to having his heart. How did you compete with a dead woman? You couldn't, and you would never win.

I could hear music playing from the wireless speaker coming from the patio. Yoshon had sent me out to run all his errands, and all I had managed to do was buy his belt and a purse he didn't authorize. Slowly walking to the patio, I watched as he smoked a blunt while listening to music from the speaker. He looked so at peace and here I was about to fuck that up by telling I bought a nearly three thousand dollar bag on his expense.

"Here's your belt," I nervously chuckled and handed him the bags.

"The fuck they give two bags for?" He put the blunt in the ash tray and leaned up. He took the boxes out the bag and opened my purse first.

"Before you open it, I'm sorry and I'll work extra hard to pay it off. I couldn't leave the store without it, and I don't want you to think that this will happen all the time. I never do things like this, and I'm so sorry. Thinking back, I should j—"

He pulled the purse out of the box. "You bought a purse? You rambling and shit like I'm 'bout to trip. It's nice; I like it," he calmly stated and placed the bag back into the box and handed it to me.

"Thank you! I'm sorry that I did that without talking to you."

"I mean, if you were my girl, you wouldn't have to keep having to apologize, but because you're my friend, you can keep the apologies coming," he smirked.

"Oh, fuck you, Yoshon." I giggled and took a seat across from him.

"Pit Pat called a little while ago... your phone off?"

"It was probably on silent. What happened? Is Gyan fine?"

"Calm it down, Worrisome Patty. She was calling to tell me that he did good in school and she's letting him eat dinner and watch TV tonight."

"Pit Pat gonna do what she want with my child anyway," I laughed.

The only reason I didn't mind Pit Pat stepping in was because I knew it was coming from a good place. How Pit Pat ran her house, I could tell she and my grandmother were the same. If my grandmother was still around, she would have been raising Gyan the same exact way. Not to mention, Gyan loved when Pit Pat stepped in with him. It was something about that old woman that he just loved. I could tell him the sky was blue and he would look at me skeptically but let Pit Pat tell him and then toss in a story about when she grew up, and he was sold. In the short amount of time, I loved how their relationship grew, and I wouldn't change it for the world. Going out of town was easier knowing someone like Pit Pat was watching over Gyan, along with security that Yoshon had hired to watch the house.

"Yeah, you know she follows her own rules. I bet your ass bought that bag and didn't do none of the shit I told you to do."

Looking down, I gave him a nervous smile. "Not exactly."

"You fine and all, but business is business. If you can't handle it, then I can hire someone that could get the job done. I play and joke all day, but when it comes to handling business, shit has to be done...feel me?"

"Yes, I hear you." How was I supposed to act like my little feelings weren't hurt? He had told me like it was and my ego was a little bruised, I could admit that. "I'll go to my bedroom to work

on the computer stuff and do better tomorrow with getting everything you asked for." I stood up and went to my bedroom.

Shutting the door, I leaned on the door and took a deep
breath. He was right. Yoshon hired me to do a job and just because
we fucked a few times didn't mean I could slack off and buy Gucci
bags just because I knew he wouldn't have a issue. He gave me an
assignment to complete and I failed. Not to mention, he told me to
email the new hires for the tanning salon the employee manual
along with their documentation to fully start, and I didn't do that.
Pulling my sneakers off, I pulled my shirt off and got right in the
middle of queen size bed. Opening my laptop, I checked and
responded to a few emails before I got right to work. Yoshon took
a chance and hired me to handle business for him, so that's what I
was going to do. I couldn't let shit let me lose focus on what I was
doing this for. Living with Yoshon wasn't a forever thing and the
plan was to get an apartment for me and Gyan.

An hour into working, my phone rang, and I answered right
away not bothering to look at the caller ID. Not too many people
had this number, so it had to be someone I had given it to.

"Hello?"

"We need to talk," Grand's voice came through the phone.
The hair on arms was at attention like they were in the damn
service.

"G...grand, what do you want from me? What I said was said,
there's nothing else you need to speak to me about."

"You send your little boyfriend to handle your business,
huh?"

"He's not my boyfriend, and I assure ain't nothing little on
him. I didn't send anybody. Just leave us alone, you've done
enough."

"I've done enough? Bitch, you had me locked up for fucking
months, facing years in prison. You lucky I'm not beating and
raping your ass some more for that high ass attorney fee I had to

pay and all the fucking bribes I had to pay out." His voice was low, but it was callous.

"I pray for your soul, Grand. I really do."

"Yeah, fucking ever. I want to see my son."

"No."

"I'll see my son if I want to. He's my son too."

"He's terrified of you, and he doesn't want to be near you at all. Don't you have other kids and women, go be with them. We're good."

"Long as you're my wife, I'm gonna be in your life. You went ahead and found you a bigger fish than me, huh? Everybody know the Santana's got money."

"It's not like that. I loved and cared for you."

"Yeah, that's what your mouth said, but your hand that you always held out for shit said otherwise," he laughed.

"I want a divorce."

"Good luck with me signing anything," he laughed and ended the call.

How did he get my number and why was he going to make this so hard? I want to be divorced from this cold and heartless monster. He didn't give a damn about anyone except himself and that was fucked up. The funny part was that he didn't give a damn about Gyan. He only wanted to use him because he knew that's the one person I cared about more than myself. Grand wanted to fuck with my emotions and get in my head. I would be the first to admit that he was good with that and it had worked in the past. Now, I had so much to work and love for, that I wasn't going to allow Grand to fuck with me and ruin what I had going on because he was miserable.

"You forgot your bag," Yoshon knocked softly and came and sat the bag onto my bed. "Somebody's busy, what you working on?" he questioned and stared at me.

"Sending out some emails and stuff. I'm getting my work done so you don't need to worry or question anything," I assured him. "I'm here to make your life easier, not harder."

"Okay, I leave you to it," he told me. "Oh, we have an appointment tomorrow morning so be ready around ten," he told me.

"Sure. I'll be ready."

After he closed the door back, I continued to work for a few until it was time to facetime with Gyan. It didn't make sense for me to inform Yoshon of Grand's call. At the end of the day, I had to be an adult and couldn't keep relying on Yoshon to fix all my issues. He had himself and his own family to worry about, not the homeless woman and her child that stayed in his guest suite.

WE SAT in a doctor's office and I wondered why we were here in the first place. Knowing Yoshon, he probably had some interest in buying into one. One of the things I loved about this man was his drive for success and building his family's wealth. He was hungry for more and more success, what he had right now wasn't enough for him. For the usual person, all he had and accomplished would be enough for them, but not for Yoshon. He had to learn more, buy more and increase his net worth more. How could you hate on a black man trying to buy property and be more to society? You couldn't; it was plain and simple. Crossing my leg, I sighed because we had been waiting for thirty minutes. After ten more minutes, a flustered white woman came rushing inside with a long, flowy, tie dyed skirt, and tank top pulled over a protruding belly.

"Yoshon, I'm so sorry. I was at prenatal yoga and lost track," she quickly apologized and then went to register at the front. *What the fuck was going on here?* Before I could even speak, she came over and told us that we could head to the back. "Ready to see your baby girl today?" she smiled at the both of us.

When I didn't smile back and stood up with my purse on my shoulder, I could read on his face that he knew I was pissed beyond measures. "Go ahead and we'll be right there in a second," he told her.

"Cool beans," she smiled and headed to the back.

"What's good with you?" He asked like he didn't know what the fuck he had just did. What did he mean what's the matter with me? If I'm correct, this man had me at the appointment with his surrogate.

"That's not fair, Yoshon," my voice cracked as I pointed at him.

"You my friend, right? Why can't you be there to support me?" he acted clueless. This man was smart and was always on point, so the fact that he was acting clueless why I was so upset, pissed me off.

"I will always support you. However, all you had to do was ask, not trick me. We're adults, not children. I have work to do so I'll be working at a Starbucks or something all day. See you at the hotel," I told him and stormed out the office. He called behind me and I continued to walk.

I literally had just found out about the baby and was still processing it. Yoshon was practically shoving the baby into my face and it wasn't fair. I had a choice, and he didn't give me one when he fed me the lie about some important business meeting I had to attend. I got into the rental and pulled out the parking lot. We drove in separate cars because he made me grab him a coffee at the appointment. Yoshon wasn't being fair with the situation. Instead of allowing me time to get used to it, he was pushing it in my face. Was it selfish that I didn't want to share him with anyone? I had finally gotten someone who was about me, and now they were being snatched away from me. Yeah, I understood that was a childish way to think, yet I couldn't stop thinking that way.

All day I ran errands and worked from my laptop. It was ten at night and I was sitting at the kitchen counter with my laptop on. Since I finished all work that needed to be done, I sat at the counter eating a burger from room service while online window shopping. I couldn't afford half the shit I put into my cart, but it was nice imagining that I could just type my card's numbers in and buy what I wanted. The front door opened and Yoshon strolled in with food from Mr. Chows. I could smell the food from the bag, and although I was smashing this burger down, I knew damn well I was going to fix me a plate of whatever he brought into this house.

"How was your day?" he broke the silence. An entire day without talking or seeing each other and I realized I was still pissed with his fine ass. How could he go ahead and try and trick me like I was some dumb chick?

"Good."

"You still mad? Let that shit go," he told me, and I gasped as he pulled the plastic containers from the paper bags.

"You have some nerve to ask me if I'm still mad. How dare you trick me and expect me to get over things?"

"I found out that I need to be in LA until Yashleigh is born. With Em being eight months approaching nine, she can come anytime."

"What does that mean for me? I have a son and can't push him to the side."

"Relax. He has his mid-winter break, so Pit Pat is flying with him here. I told Yolani to come too because I need to break this to everyone at the same time, and the phone isn't a good place to tell them."

"Gyan has school. His mid-winter break could come and go, and she still doesn't have the baby. My son's education is important to me."

"I have tutors that will coordinate with his teachers back home. Fuck, Golden. All I need is fucking support, and you're finding everything in your power to be fucking negative, man!" he barked and slammed his hand on the granite. I jumped and stared at him. "You needed a place; I did that. You needed a job; I did that. The one thing I need right now is support, and I'm not asking it to come from you as my girl, but as my fucking friend, man! People always worried about themselves!" he continued and left the counter. His bedroom door slammed soon after that.

I should have gone after him and apologized, but my ass went exploring through the bags while thinking about what he said. As much as I didn't want to admit it, he was right. As a woman, welcoming a child into the world was the most scariest, yet rewarding thing in the world. Our nature instincts kicked in and for a moment, everything felt like it was about to be alright. Thinking to myself, I could only imagine the stress that Yoshon was going through with all of this. No matter how I may have personally felt, I should have been there for him as a friend, not complaining. Since I met this man, he has never let a complaint come out of his mouth. He was content with helping others and here I was being a selfish bitch because he was upfront with me about his situation. He could have lied to me and he didn't. Instead, he was truthful and told me what I needed to hear.

God was pushing me to go and apologize, and I knew I had to, so I fixed both of us a plate and walked into his room. He was smoking weed on the patio, which extended to his side of the suite.

"I brought you some food."

"Not hungry," he quickly replied while puffing his blunt.

"After that, you'll be. We need to talk, Yoshon."

"On the real, I'm tired of fucking talking. We're good. I heard you loud and clear," he told me and it hurt me that I had hurt him. He needed me, and I let him down, which was fucked up.

"I'm sorry. Yes, I'm a selfish, homeless bitch who thinks of herself and son. You needed me, and I was so focused on my personal feelings that I couldn't see that you needed me as a friend. I apologize about that, and I promise to be there for you as a friend. You're about to be a dad, and that's the most rewarding and scariest thing you'll do in your life." I sat our plates down and then went to climb in his lap. He allowed me to climb in his lap and continued to smoke. If I was him, I would have pushed my ass right off of me.

"You apologizing? Hmph."

"Don't do me, Yoshon. I can admit when I'm wrong and I'm dead wrong. I thought about it, and it's not about if we're together or not, it's about you adjusting to being a father."

"I want us together."

"How do you know? Things will change when your daughter gets here."

"Why the fuck are you intimidated by a baby that's not even in the world? Fuck is up, Golden?"

He was right. I was intimidated by a little girl who couldn't talk, walk or feed herself. "My fear is that if we ever get so serious, where we want to have kids that our kids won't mean the same. Yashleigh means a lot to you, not only because she's your child, but because she's the only thing you have of Ashleigh. What if our children we have together don't equal up? What if she hates me because she thinks I'm trying to be her mother? It's a lot, Yoshon."

"Does Gyan hate me? I mean, do I walk around and try to be his pops? I know I'm not his pops and so does he. We have a mutual respect, and you and Yashleigh will have the same. It'll be kind of hard for her to feel ill towards you when you've been there since she was born. Ashleigh is a part of her, yes. However, she's a stranger to her just like she is to you. All she'll know is that Ashleigh is her mother. I could tell her all I want about her mother, but she'll never witness or experience the beautiful soul her mother was."

"Yoshon, you haven't gotten over Ashleigh. My fear is that I'm stepping in on another's woman's territory. She still has your heart, dead or alive."

"I'm not going to lie to you because I'm always going to keep it real with you. Ashleigh will always have a piece of my heart because I lost her prematurely. I've had time to mourn and try to move on, and that's what I'm doing with you. Golden, you came into my life and fucking turned shit around for me. I want to spend every waking moment with you and Gyan; y'all dead ass make me feel complete. Hearing his feet running through the house in the morning or hearing Pit Pat wake him up in the morning makes me fucking smile while lying in bed. Our home had been quiet as shit with just the two of us and look at it now. Pit Pat loves having you both there with us, and she don't like people in her crib. I want this. I want us. I just need to know that you want the same things so I'm not wasting my time," he held my face as he spoke right to me.

This was the thing with being with a grown ass man. Yoshon wasn't like Grand; he wasn't young and stupid, he was grown. He proved how grown he was over and over again. Where he could have lied to me, he didn't. Even if he knew it would hurt me, he was honest with me. How could I not appreciate that coming from a man?

"I do want this. I'm just...scared." I sighed and held my head down.

A part of me was terrified to start to love this man. He was the real deal and I didn't want to fuck up things with him. Not to mention, he wasn't here for my young ass behavior. As much as I was mature, I had the moments when I did act like my age. Yoshon wasn't with the kiddy games and being with him meant that I had to step my game up as well.

"Scared of what, baby? I'd tell you the truth before I ever hurt you. I'm transparent, what you see is what you'll get."

"Okay, Jellyfish," I giggled to lighten the mood.

"On the real, I want to be with you. I want to help you raise Gyan and be happy. If that's not what you want, let me know now so I can get over my feelings for you."

"I want us." I smiled and kissed him on the lips.

"Since you wanna be shopping in Gucci and shit, and only

bring me back a belt... I'm taking you to dinner and some shopping," he told me.

"We have dinner already. You don't need to take me shopping; I'm happy with the bag."

"Nah, since you wanted to be on Rodeo Drive, I'm about to really show you Rodeo Drive," He smirked and gripped my ass.

"If you insist. I'm excited to have my baby here with me. I want to take him to Disney land while we're here."

"We can do that."

"I don't expect you to come with us. I know you have stuff that needs to be done and we don't wan—"

"Golden, shut up. I want to go and have fun with y'all. Stop fronting on me, ight."

"Yeah, whatever," I smiled.

The sun was setting, and we were looking at the beautiful view while being cuddled on the patio. It felt right sitting here with him. "You sleeping in my bed tonight?"

"Nope," I smirked.

"Yeah, ight. Your thick ass will be right in my bed. You want this dick." He held his dick print and my mouth watered. He was right. I wanted that dick more than I wanted this food from Mr. Chows.

Before he was able to get my ass to his room with my legs up, I asked him a question I should have been asked. "How was the appointment?"

"You sure you want to know?"

"I wouldn't be asking unless I was, babe."

"It was good. Lil' mama is growing and is at seven pounds already. She's coming so it's about making Em comfortable, but she's been doing yoga, eating right and all that white people shit. I really appreciate her for taking pride in this pregnancy like it was her own child she was carrying."

"How do you feel. This is the home stretch now." I knew he felt nervous and was probably panicking more than what he was showing. It was fine for him to be nervous. He was about to be a father to a little girl that would spend her entire life looking up to her father. He would be her entire world, especially since she didn't have a mother there to look up to.

"I'm nervous about talking to Pit Pat. I know she gonna be in her feelings about me keeping it a secret."

Touching his shoulder, I offered him a smile. "Your grand-mother loves and supports anything that any of her grandchil-dren does. She'll understand your reason for keeping mute on the situation. She'll also step in and raise her great-grandchild as well." I rubbed his head and he looked to be lost in his thoughts. "And, I'll also be there for you too."

He looked up and paused his thoughts for a second. "Golden, I don't want you to feel like I'm forcing to be a part of something you're not ready for. I had a minute to think and it was selfish of me to trick you into coming to the appointment. It was some childish shit and it will never happen again."

"Yes, it was childish. What was fucked up was me not wanting to be a part. You're a part of my son's life every day and never complain. In fact, you're happy to be a part of his life which means that much more to me." I smiled and held his face.

This was different and I was, of course, scared. Still, what if he was scared to lend a hand and help me and my son that night? Where would we be now? I knew he would need help, and he couldn't do this without a support system. Yoshon was a good person and it didn't take me long to figure that out. He deserved to have the same support he had been giving me since he met me in the middle of the blizzard.

7

Hazel

MY MOTHER CALLED my cell phone for the sixth time since she had got up this morning. I hadn't had morning sickness at all, and then it came out of nowhere. The thing that confused me was that it happened at night or early evening. Some nights I couldn't make it out of bed and had to use the trash can beside my bed. I loved my parents more than life and appreciated them welcoming me home with open arms, except they had a boatload of questions I wasn't ready to answer yet. How was I going to explain everything to them and I was still confused about a bunch of stuff? Here I was a successful business owner knocked up, living in my parent's house and dealing with a fake wife who had a drug problem? Why did this happen to me? I was a good person, paid my taxes and brushed my teeth three times a day. So, why was all of this happening to me at one time?

"I know you saw my call come through on your phone," my mother finally successfully picked the lock to my bedroom door.

"Get some clothes and fix yourself up. Alicia is downstairs in the living room with her boyfriend," she told me like I gave a shit about my cousin.

Alicia always had some new damn boyfriend that she wanted to parade around here like we gave a shit. My parents always entertained her and hosted dinners, which is another reason I rarely came home. Alicia's parents died when we were sixteen years old. They died in a car accident trying to make it home from a conference they attended out of town. She moved in with us and then moved out when she was eighteen with some boyfriend at the time. My parents were the closest thing she had to parents, and I didn't mind sharing them. The one thing I hated about my parents was that they didn't approve of me being gay but supported Alicia anytime she had a new boyfriend. It was known that Alicia got around with niggas that only had money. She was always with some nigga that had money and was flaunting him around. Mind you, she was unemployed and lived with whoever she was with at the time.

"I'm not hungry and I'm not in the mood to deal with her new boyfriend for the week." My mother rolled her eyes and held on to the door.

"I wasn't asking. Since you been here, all do you is lay up in this room all day throwing up. You don't come and spend no time with me or your father. You pregnant, ain't you?" she suspected right away.

"Ma, just because I don't want to sit and play nice at dinner doesn't mean I'm pregnant."

"I'm no fool, Hazel. You're barely eating, and when you do eat, you're vomiting. You spend most of the days sleeping all damn day and never going to your shop. I know when a woman is knocked up," she accused. "You better not be so stupid to get pregnant with that woman," she spat as she left the room.

"Whatever," I rolled my eyes and tried to turn over, and she pulled the blanket off my body. "Ma, give me the blanket."

"Go ahead and put some clothes on. I'm not about to play with you, and if you don't get up and come down, you can find somewhere else to live. Oh, and we'll be having a discussion. Your father might be blind and think you came home because life got too hard, but I'm no fool." She waved her hand at me and left my room.

Sitting up, I rolled my eyes and looked at my ringing cell phone. It was Denim calling again and I ignored it – again. He had been calling me all the damn time and I continued to ignore his calls. I needed to sort things out before we sat down and had a conversation. Denim thought that he could whisk himself into town and I would automatically leave Yolani and my life like it didn't matter. I had a lot to think about before leaving her and moving on with him. That was even if I wanted to leave Yolani. She needed me. How could I leave her and not get her help? I owed this to Pit Pat more than I owed it to Yolani's ass. Picking myself up, I switched into a maxi dress and some white cotton socks and headed down the hall to wash my face and comb my hair. They were lucky that I was blessing them with my appearance, so they was about to get this comfortable ass attire I had on.

"Auntie, you know I was craving your ribs. Right, babe, I was talking about them," Alicia's annoying voice sounded as I came down the stairs.

She was with some bearded brown skin dude who was holding her hand. "Nice of you to join us, Hazel," my mother sarcastically remarked.

"Hey," I said to Alicia dryly.

"Hey cousin. I came by the shop so you could hook me up, but you weren't there. Can you hook me up tonight?" she asked. Alicia always came to the salon and never paid. She thought because we were family that she could come in without scheduling an appointment and not pay full price. The type of nails she got cost over a hundred dollars, and she would toss fifty dollars like it would cover her service.

"No. I have a shop where you can pay full price for your nails."

"Haze, money isn't an issue," she giggled, clearly embarrassed in front of her friend.

"Oh yeah? Explains why you gave me less money last time I did your nails," I chuckled and went over to the new man in her life. "How are you? I'm Hazel."

"Grand," he shook my hand back.

"Your father is running late so we'll start dinner early. Come into the dining room. I spent all morning cooking," my mother smiled.

We all made our way to the dining area and I sat Indian style in the chair. My mother brought out our plates and sat them down. My mother always had this thing for entertaining. Well, except when me and Yolani visited. Yolani hated to visit my parents and I never blamed her. My parents didn't like her; they tolerated her. When we came over, my mother didn't bother to cook and was always in bed. It was my father she left to cover up with some bullshit excuse.

"So, how long have you two been dating?" my mother questioned and started to eat her food. My father was the one who always said grace, so I knew she wouldn't do it unless he was home.

"We've been dating for three months. I went to Virginia with a few girls for a concert and ran right into him. Of course, he had a girlfriend at the time, but she wasn't worth nothing because look where he is now."

"I hear that, Alicia. You know how we Brown women are," my mother referred to herself by her maiden name for a quick moment.

"Yes, Auntie... Anyway, we have been tight ever since. He didn't want to come to New York, and I had to keep traveling to Virginia to see him. He finally made the move to come up here and stay with me."

"Stop with all that," he squeezed her shoulder gently. "I had something to wrap up before I could make it up this way. I was outgrowing Virginia anyway."

"Wait, you moved here for her?" I just had to know the answer to my question. It looked like for once Alicia found her a keeper.

"Yes. Especially since we're expecting!" she squealed in excitement.

My mother dropped her fork and I got excited because for once Alicia was about to hear my mother's roar. "Omg! Are you serious, Alicia? I'm about to be a great aunt!" she clapped her hands excitedly.

"Wait What?" I blurted, confused by her act of excitement. "How the hell are you excited? You know this will last a few seconds and then she'll be on your door pregnant with no job. Yet, you scoffed at me when you accused me of being pregnant upstairs?"

"Hazel, this isn't the time." She cut her eyes at me angrily. She was pissed that I was putting her on the spot.

"Well, I'm pregnant too," I announced since everyone had an announcement in this bitch. I had one and I wanted my mother to know about it too.

"How stupid could you be? That damn woman runs around and does what she wants, and you're carrying a child by her?" my mother shouted, forgetting that we had company.

"You forget she doesn't have a dick? I'm surprised you did because you don't waste time to call out that she's a woman," I replied calmly and took a spoonful of potatoes into my mouth.

"Hazel, how stupid could you have been?" she pushed herself away from the table. "A baby? Do you know what that means?"

"Yeah, it means the same thing that it does for Alicia, I'm having a baby. What the fuck makes me so different? I have my own business, money in my account and I'm able to take care of myself and a child."

"Yet, you laid around this damn house like a damn bum. Not

going to work and laying around here like a damn piece of the furniture." She had the nerve to say to me.

I haven't been myself the past few days, and I had been laying around while feeling sorry for myself. Even with me laying around, I was still making money while laying around. With all this happening, the first place I thought to come was home. I complained about my parents, but I didn't want to be in a hotel, I wanted to be home. She damn near dropped her silverware to be excited for Alicia, but when I mention that I'm pregnant, she's upset and calling me out of my name. The shit was fucked up and I was used to it. My mother always babied Alicia. I guess it was because she lost her parents young and she felt she needed to make her feel included in our small family. I didn't mind having my cousin live with us and share my parents; it was how my parents acted that caused me not to fuck with my cousin. She saw the shit and never said shit, instead, she soaked up all the attention like the big-headed whore she was.

"Okay guys let's not do this in front of Grand. Congratulations, cousin. I hope we have girls," she smiled. From her face, I could tell that Alicia was excited for me.

"Thank you. I'd rather a boy."

"I'd rather you not have any damn child," my mother mumbled as she started to eat her food again.

Pushing my plate back, I stood up and left the dining room. It was a part of the reason that I didn't come and spend time with her ass. Mo always told me that I was rude and mean to my mother, but she didn't see the shit she did. Every decision I've ever made in my life was never good enough for her. I went to nail school, made money doing nails out the basement and then opened a successful shop. None of those things were good enough for her. She felt I should have been going to college to be a lawyer or something with substance. So, instead of trying to make her proud of my career choice, I chose to make her proud of my personal life, and she didn't support or agree with that. No matter what, I tried to make my mother proud, and it was never enough for her. It wasn't enough that I was a successful business owner who had the money to take care of myself. I didn't need Yolani; I wanted to be with her. My parents didn't see that. It was more my mother than my father. He checked on me and tried to understand my relationship with Yolani. The sad part was that I wanted to make my mother proud. I wanted to hear her say how proud she was of me, and I would never hear that out of her mouth.

I closed and locked the room door back and climbed back into the bed. Staying here for too much longer wasn't going to be an option. The last thing I wanted to do was to rent a apartment, and I didn't want to go back to the home I shared with Yolani. The only option I could think of was staying in a hotel. My mother made me feel like I wasn't wanted home. Here I was knocked up, lonely and being made out to be the fuck up of the family. I knew one thing, I needed to get out of this house because my mother was going to drive me up the damn wall.

There was a knock at the door, and I looked at the door and tried to act as if I didn't hear it. The person knocked once more, and this time I heard Alicia's voice. "I know you hear me, Hazel," she spoke through the door.

Rolling my eyes, I unlocked and opened my bedroom door. "What?"

Alicia pushed her way into the room and I closed the door back. "I'm sorry about, Auntie. I didn't know you were pregnant. If I would have known, I wouldn't have said anything," she apologized. As much as I couldn't stand my cousin, this wasn't her fault. She didn't make my mother say all those things, and she damn sure didn't make my mother act the way she acted toward me.

"It's fine. I'm used to what comes out my mother's mouth by now."

"It's not okay. I don't really say anything because last time I did, she cursed me out and told me that it wasn't my business what happened between you and her," she revealed to me. All this time I thought my cousin didn't speak up because she didn't care. Finding out she had been on the receiving end of my mother's lethal tongue surprised me. My mother was the sweetest woman in the world, but she had the nastiest tongue and attitude when it was something she didn't like.

"Alicia, my mother has been doing this my entire life. Since I started making my own decisions, she hasn't been happy. I'm not surprised now, just disappointed."

"You and Yolani went to the sperm bank to make this happen?" she questioned. I knew that was a question my mother wanted to know as well.

"No, it's Denim's baby."

"Denim?" she gasped. "First of all, when did he come back into town and how did that happen? Is he like your sperm donor or something?"

"No, we've been fucking around, and that's how this happened," I pointed at my stomach. I didn't have a stomach yet, but I knew in the short amount of time that I would be showing. My stomach was flat, so I knew I would be looking bloated soon, but would actually be pregnant.

"Auntie know? She loves Denim."

"Nope."

"I'll keep my mouth shut; you don't need to worry about that," she promised. Alicia was good with keeping her mouth shut. I knew she wouldn't say anything to my mother about who I was pregnant by.

"Thank you. How did this happen?"

"I really like him, cuz. He's so sweet and rough around the edges. He's moving to New York but plans to be back and forth."

"Okay, I'm happy for you and hope it lasts."

"So do I. I'm pregnant and ready to be a wife. I'm not trying to be someone's baby mama for the rest of my life."

"I feel you."

"Speaking of being pregnant by Denim, what's going on with Yolani?"

"Me and her aren't legally married and she's been on her own time. We're taking a break and trying to figure things out."

"Wait, not legally married?"

"Yep. I've got too much stuff going on to deal with Yolani and her bullshit," I rolled my eyes. "I'm too busy trying to keep this food down and deal with my mother."

"We have a spare room in our condo. I don't mind you coming to stay with us for a while. Grand is between here and Virginia, and I'm here all day with nothing to do."

As tempting as Alicia's offer was, I would be damned if I went and lived with her. I would go and get my own apartment before I moved in with my cousin. She forgot that we had to live together for two years and it was hell. The girl is sloppy and inconsiderate to people's property. It was the same reason that I didn't allow her to move in with me when she was kicked out of her friend's house. Me and her couldn't live under the same roof. When we were younger, we had no choice. Now that I was a grown ass woman, I had a choice, and my choice wasn't to live with her ass.

"I'm fine. I'll probably start apartment hunting or something." I didn't know if I wanted an apartment alone just yet. It was something that I had been thinking about. Moving in alone meant that this was real. Me and Yolani weren't together, and I was going to be moving on without her. When I said my vows, I meant them. It was her who was deceiving and didn't keep it real with me from the start.

"If you need help, let me know. I'm always bored in the house when Grand is away."

"I will," I lied again.

Now that she knew we were both pregnant, she was going to make sure we spent as much time together, and I wasn't pleased. My cousin wasn't that bad; I just preferred to be alone half the time. I was a only child and used to my solitude. Alicia stayed in my room for a bit before she hugged me bye and went back downstairs to talk to my mother. Soon as she closed the door, I locked it and climbed back into bed with the taste of those ribs on my tongue.

TODAY WAS THE DAY. I finally pulled myself out the bed, combed my hair and had a decent outfit on. My mother had gone to work early so my dad was just home. I wasn't too sure if he had work today or if he was off. For most of the morning, I sat in bed and handled business from my laptop. The sun was peeking out and I was desperate to get out of the house. After spending almost two weeks in the house, I needed to get out of this house and feel some air on my skin. I've always been the type that got stir crazy when left in the house for too long. My mother had made enough smart remarks since the dinner to convince me that I needed to get out from under her roof. Whenever we were both in the same room of the house, she would have a smart remark that would piss me off. If it was any other person, I would have cussed them out into next Tuesday. Except, it was my mother, and I couldn't unleash all these years of hurt and anger at her.

"Hey, baby girl. What you up to today?" My father questioned when he saw me come into the kitchen.

"I'm going to the shop to check on everyone, and then going to look at a few apartments with a realtor."

"Realtor? Baby girl, you don't need to leave so soon. We're not pushing you out," he took a sip of his morning coffee. "It's just me and your mama, so we actually like the company."

"Daddy, I believe it when it comes from you, but with mama, I don't believe it. She goes out of her way to tell me how displeased she is with my pregnancy. Why do you allow her to pull you into what she doesn't like?"

"When you've been married as long as we have, you compromise, babe. I don't agree with everything your mother does, but a happy wife is a happy life."

"Even with your own child?" There was no need for me to go back and forth with my father.

My mother had always made it easy for my father. She's always made home his escape when he came through those pine-oak doors. It didn't matter that she worked too, dinner was always on the table, and his shower was running soon after he finished, followed by a beer on the sitting room end table. My father had it made when it came to having to step in to raise me. I was a self-sufficient child and pretty much did everything on my own. My mother did her job as a mother and my father footed the bill. Why go against the woman that runs your entire life where you never have a care in the world? He never did when I was a teen, and I didn't expect him to do it with me being an adult.

"Hazel, you and your mother have had this tit for tat relationship your entire life. One minute you are both fine, then the next you're not. What is going on now?"

"Besides the fact that I'm pregnant."

"She did mention it to me the other night. I was so consumed with the tennis match I didn't pay her any mind. Are you pregnant or not?"

"I am."

"By Yolani... I'm not sure how it works, Hazel. You know I'm trying," he chuckled, and I laughed too as I pulled a seat up across from him.

"I know you are, Daddy. I didn't tell mama, but it's by Denim. Me and Yolani has been going through some issues and I slipped up with Denim."

"Denim's back into town. Ro-Ro didn't tell me," he called Denim's mother by her nickname. Every adult called her by that name, and if you didn't, it meant that you weren't close to her.

"He came back to open another one of his shops. We had

dinner together and..." My voice trailed off because it was embarrassing to talk to my dad about cheating on my wife.

"Then that baby came. I don't like how the baby came about, but I am happy to be having a grandchild soon." He smiled and touched my hand.

"Thanks, Dad. I'm happy someone is excited because I'm nervous."

"Me and your mama were scared when she found out she was pregnant with you. We worried about a bunch of stuff you don't need to worry about. You're successful, and that baby will be loved from us and from you. Not to mention, I know Denim will be excited to be a father."

"We still haven't had a conversation on how this is going to work between us," I sighed. "Dad, being an adult is hard."

"Well, you're about to be an adult and a mother, so that's even harder," he cracked a smile. "Go on about your day. I need to go get ready for work anyway." He stood up, drained the remainder of his coffee into the sink and came to kiss me on the forehead.

"Thank you for the chat, Dad." I smiled.

"Anytime, baby. I wished you would come out that room more often, but I understand why." He winked and went upstairs to his bedroom.

After having a quick chat with my father, I felt good about things, and I knew I now needed to have a conversation with Denim. We needed to figure out what we were going and how we were going to move forward with everything pertaining to this baby. I knew he wanted to talk about us and we were going with our relationship, but right now wasn't the time for that. I had a gut filled with his baby, and I didn't need to be thinking of a relationship with Denim. Especially with everything that was going on with Yolani. Yolani was stubborn so when she stopped calling, I knew she was not officially in her feelings. She felt like she wasn't about to kiss my ass, even if she was the one that fucked up. Grabbing a bottled water, my keys and purse, I headed to

Denim's apartment. My wheels should have been going in the opposite direction, not to his home.

Denim was a good man, and if I had to have a baby by anyone, I was glad it was him. It wasn't the fact that he could provide for both me and the baby. It was about him being a good man, morally. He took care of his daughter and never talked bad about his baby mother, even though I had heard him argue with her a few times. He never got off the phone and bad mouthed her. Instead, he would state how he knew he had some fault in the argument. If there was a perfect man, it would be Denim. Except, I felt like I didn't deserve a man like him. I was a filthy slut who fucked him bareback and ended up pregnant while supposed to be married to someone else. How did a woman like me, land a man like him?

My wheels pulled in front of his apartment building and I killed my engine. I was scared to come face to face with him. I had blew up on him and stormed out of his store last time we spoke. He told me about Yolani not being my wife, so how did he think I would react? He dropped a huge bomb after I found out that I was carrying a little bomb made by his ass. It didn't take me long to make it to the front of his door. This was crazy; I didn't even know if he was home or not. Usually, I would know where he was, but I had made it a point not to give a shit. When I locked myself in my parent's house, I stopped trying to keep up with everybody. Mo had been the only person I spoke to, and that was because she pushed herself into my bedroom and threatened to key my car if I didn't open the door for her.

"Hazel, you good?" He opened his eyes. I hadn't realized I've been standing there in my own thoughts that I didn't knock on the door. Denim was wearing a duffle bag on his shoulder and looked as if he was going on vacation or something.

"I... we need to talk," I stammered. His sudden presence had me at a loss for words. Denim had me wanting to wrap him up in my legs like I have plenty of times before.

"Ight. About what?" He stood there like he didn't even want to let me inside his place. Was I subject to conversations in the hallway now?

"Well, I wanted to talk about how we're going to co-parent with the baby and stuff like that." When I mentioned the baby, his face softened.

"Come in." was all he said and stepped away from the door to allow me to walk inside. I walked inside clutching my purse and sat on his couch. This place looked the same and smelled the same. It was as if no time had passed and everything in his house was exactly the same. Nothing was out of place like always. "What you want to talk about?"

"This baby," I choked out. "I'm scared and I have the support of no one. How am I going to have this baby without any support?"

"You have my support, and you already know my moms is going to be there for us too. I'm not trying to have you go through this alone, Hazel. I went half on this baby with you and I want to be here to help you go through everything."

"I'm just so confused, Denim. You're who I can talk to about everything I've just been holding it all in," I wept.

He placed his bag down and came and comforted me on the couch. Rubbing my shoulders, he kissed my forehead and allowed me to cry and complain about everything. "Stop crying because it's not like you got pregnant by a nigga that's not shit. I'm gonna hold you down, even though you don't need me to hold you down."

"I just want you to know that I love you. My feelings I feel for you aren't a game. I don't want to hurt you, Denim. My life is complicated, and I can't tell you how many times I just want to toss in the towel with Yolani and start over with you, but I can't. I can't leave the relationship with her and jump straight with you and hand you all the issues I have."

"I'm not asking you to do that. All I want is for you to choose what's right for you. If you feel like making your marriage work is the key, then I had no choice but to support that. Long as Yolani can respect my role as the father of your child, then I can respect her role as the stepmother to my child."

This man was so fucking mature and it was so foreign to hear these words come out his mouth. If this was Yolani, she would have been cursing and being immature about the entire situation. Denim was sitting here giving me his blessings to go and make things work with Yolani if that's what I wanted to do. Deep down, it wasn't what I wanted to do at all. I didn't want to be with Yolani and raise my child. I wanted to be with Denim and raise our child together. At first, I didn't know what I wanted to do, but I wanted to be with him, and I wanted to be his real wife this time.

"I want to be with you, Denim," I told him.

"Haze, you just saying that shit. We can talk about this when I get back. I got a bachelor party to go to in Vegas, and I'm a day late since I had the grand opening to the shop," he told me.

I was supposed to be there to cheer him on at his grand opening and I wasn't. Too busy stuck in my ways, I wasn't there for him like I should have been. "Sorry."

"You're good. There will be others, and you'll make those, I'm sure of it," he winked.

"Marry me, Denim. Take me to Vegas and let's get married," I blurted, unsure of what the hell I was doing right about now. All I was doing was being impulsive, and for the first time, I didn't feel like it was a bad thing or that I was making a bad decision. My chest heaved up and down, and I gripped the side of my pants like my life depended on it, yet I didn't take back the words I had spat out previously.

"Hazel, if you don't go home and rest," he chuckled and waved it off. When he realized, I was serious, and I hadn't moved, cracked a smile or even tried to breathe, he stopped smiling.

"You serious?"

"I am. We didn't do what we were supposed to do years ago.

Life separated us and we were supposed to be together. God made all of this happen and who are we to not do something about it? This baby, us falling in love – all of this."

He stood there and didn't know what to do. I watched as he ran his hand across his face a few times as he was debating with himself. "You crazy as shit," he laughed and rushed over to me and picked me up. "But, you already know I don't love it unless it's a little crazy." He kissed me on the lips as he held me up in the middle of the living room.

"I love you, Denim." For once, I was doing something that I wanted to for myself. I wasn't listening to anyone else, except my heart.

8

Yolani

WORD AROUND TOWN was that Cherry's hoe ass had gotten out the hospital. She was so bad that they had to release her to her sister's house with nurses that cleaned her wounds. The last thing I needed was to go over and see her, so I booked a flight to the west coast like Yoshon had requested. He claimed he had some big thing he needed to talk to me about. If it gave me more money, then I was jumping my ass on a plane to find out what he needed to tell me. Hazel's ass had been gone and hadn't even called me. I wasn't surprised; she felt like she was owed an apology. Neither of us were angels in this, and we both needed to come together and fix this shit before it was too late. I loved my wife and a paper didn't change that shit. Hazel got caught up on the wrong things. She was so busy worried about a damn paper instead of being the wife of someone as big as I was. She had any and everything she could think of. Instead of being grateful that she lived in a beautiful home, had a foreign car and had a successful nail shop because of me wasn't enough for her.

Then she had to be the one to go ahead and fuck another nigga behind my back. Yeah, I wasn't a saint, and I did shit the way I wanted during our relationship, but did she have to do a nigga like that? I grabbed my duffle bag and exited off the plane. Yoshon didn't need much, but when he did, I made sure I came through for him. It had been a while since me and my brother kicked it. I lowkey was praying this wasn't some intervention. Knowing Hazel, her big mouth ass probably spilled all my business to Yoshon and Pit Pat. At the end of the day I'm a grown ass bitch and if I want to dabble in some drugs, I can. She was acting like I was scratching and begging for another hit or something. My ass was chilling and getting high when I had some downtime and shit.

It didn't take me no time to make it through the airport and wait outside. Yoshon told me he was going to pick me up from the airport. After waiting a few minutes, I saw a Rolls Royce pull up to pick up area. A group of boys were all hype about the whip and it was regular shit to me. Yoshon got out and wrapped me in his arms.

"Damn, felt like I haven't seen you in forever, baby sis." He grabbed my duffle bag and placed it in the back seat.

"Business is taking all of my time and shit," I got into the front of the car. He slipped behind the wheel and pulled off. "Why the hell you out here in Cali? What's up?"

"In due time you'll find out," he spoke in codes and shit. This nigga needed to tell me why the fuck I was out here. Did he have a new business venture with the drugs and needed me to move out here to oversee it?

"Cut the small talk. Why the fuck you move all the traps and got Grape not telling me where they are?" I cut to the chase. That was the real reason my ass was on that plane this morning to find out why the fuck he made a move like that. Yoshon wasn't interested in the drug operation and handed that to me with pride. Now, he wanted to step in and make moves. I had to fuck up three of my soldiers, and those tough niggas still wouldn't tell me what the hell I wanted to know.

"I knew you came too easy," he smirked. "You got too much on your shoulders and I'm reliving the pressure."

"I'm good. I've always been good when it comes to handling business with the streets."

"Nah, you haven't. You always put the streets before your wife and your home."

"Hazel ain't an issue anymore." It seemed that big mouth hadn't opened her mouth, so I was able to sway things to work in my favor.

"What you mean she's not your issue anymore? The fuck is up with y'all?"

"She found out that we weren't legally married. It slipped my mind to go and file those papers. Shit, maybe it didn't slip my mind, I was scared to make a commitment."

"Damn, you gonna regret losing her. Hazel's a good woman, Lani. You don't find women like that walking around every day, feel me?"

"Yeah, whatever. There's a dozen of women I could call and would fill her shoes without the nagging."

"When women nag, they love you. It's when they stop the nagging that you should be worried. Do you, it's your life, and I'm not going to get involved in that shit."

"Good. Now, tell me where my traps are so I could catch a flight out of here tomorrow morning and get back to business."

"Nah." Was all he said as he continued to drive through Beverly Hills.

California was somewhere I didn't mind laying down some roots. I've ran through mostly all the women in New York; maybe I needed to change my surroundings. Get me a house out in Malibu and live my life to the fullest. Hazel thought she was doing something to me by leaving. Nah, she was doing me a favor by going about her business. She would realize she fucked up and came home, so I wasn't worried. This wasn't the first time that Hazel fled from our home for a few days or even a week. Usually, she went to Mo's crib, but this time her ass went home. It wouldn't be too long before her ass ended up back on my doorstep begging to for me to let her in so we could talk about shit. I probably could forgive her for fucking with that nigga. Especially if she came home, it would only prove that she wanted to come right where she belonged, and that nigga was only to be used for what he had– dick.

"I got you a suite on the same floor as us. Pit Pat is staying in the suite with me and Golden."

"Oh, you got your shorty here?" I hadn't met the infamous Golden that had my brother out here all in love. Pit Pat informed me of her when she stayed at my crib, but she didn't get too much into her.

"Yeah, if you came around, you would have been met her," he snickered and got out the car while the valet patiently waited for the keys.

"Man, I be busy. You always got some women that you serious about. The fuck happened to Eva's fine ass?"

"Me and her weren't together; we were kicking it."

"Kicking it, eh? You was busting that woman's cheeks, and she was breaking her damn neck to come and chill at your crib whenever you called."

"Just like you were kicking it with all your bitches. That's exactly what the fuck I've been doing." The doors were held open as we walked inside the hotel.

"Chill. Those women were friends. I told Hazel that and I'm telling you that. Why be shackled down when we can be single? We can have a bunch of women," I tried to convince him. After Ashleigh passed, I told him he should get out there and thot around. He didn't need to be held up in the crib acting like he was a grandpa. From living with Pit Pat, his ass had developed into an old ass person.

"That's the thing; I never feel shackled up. Stop looking at a relationship and commitment as slavery. A woman being in your life is there to bring you to new heights as a person. You too busy thinking about being tied down."

"Yeah, whatever. You saw how extra Hazel's ass was."

"You not about to fight for your woman?"

"Hell nah. If she wanna come home, she can come back. I'm not chasing or kissing no damn ass. Her ass wanna act all innocent while she fucking her ex-nigga who came back into town."

"Hmph." Was all he said.

"You knew about this?"

"Nah. I just knew she was going to step out on the relationship soon. Me and Pit Pat had bet some money on it too, and she owes me two hundred dollars."

"The fuck? Y'all betting on my relationship ending. Where the fuck is the faith, man?"

"Nigga, you didn't even have faith in your own relationship, so how did you expect someone else to?"

He put the keycard into his hotel suite and opened the door. When I walked in, some thick brown skin chick was stretching on the patio. I could see how fat that ass was like I had X-ray vision. Yoshon turned and stared at me before he spoke.

"Stop eye-fucking my girl," he sternly warned me.

Golden smiled when she saw both of us enter the suite. Walking through the door, she tossed the towel in her hand over her shoulder with a bright smile on her face. "Hey, I'm Golden. It's finally nice to meet you, Yolani." She came and hugged me.

"What's good? Nice to finally meet the woman that got my brother over here skipping and shit." We broke our embrace and Yoshon wrapped his arms around her waist, and she leaned into him.

"Stop fronting. I ain't skipping."

"Oh no? I almost felt special knowing you were skipping," she giggled. "You'll probably see my son run through here with Pit Pat soon. They're at the pool," she informed me.

"Oh word. You got a seed too?"

"Yes. Can I get you anything?"

"Nah, I'm about to head to my room and take a nap. I had an early morning today and want to nap before hitting the night scene. Y'all coming out tonight?"

"I don't do the club," Yoshon was the first to speak. He didn't fuck around with clubs even when he was younger.

"I do. I'll come out with you. We can get to know each other more," Golden suggested.

"Bet. I'll come and get you later tonight." I nodded and headed out the door. The real reason I wanted to head out tonight was because I wanted to see who could get me some coke. The club was where I could find any damn drug I pleased. I started to ask my friend to charter his jet, but I didn't have enough time.

Soon as I got into my suite, I kicked my kicks off and sat on the edge of the bed. Staring at my phone, I had no missed calls from Hazel. She was pissing me the fuck off with being stubborn. Signing onto Instagram, I went to her page and saw she had uploaded her first picture in weeks. It was a picture of a plane's wing with the caption. *You're about to take me to new heights.* What the fuck she meant by you're about to take me to new heights, and where the fuck was she going? If I knew something, then I knew that Yoshon probably had her coming out here anyway, and I would be seeing her when she landed. He got me a big ass suite, so she was about to be here soon. I got on the bed and laid back to catch a nap before I had to hear her big ass mouth. Right now, the silence was well welcomed as I slipped off to sleep in the middle of the king size bed.

9

Yoshon

IT WAS three in the morning when Golden came into the bedroom. She had her heels in one hand and looked to be pissed in the face. I was sitting up in the bed watching some documentary I had found on Netflix. I was always one to keep my mind growing so I would rather watch something educational than something that I felt like I was losing IQ points over. Gyan had just went to sleep two hours before since we were playing the game. Once I saw it was getting too late, I sent him off to bed. He and Pit Pat were sharing a room. I offered to get Pit Pat her own room, but she insisted that she stay with us and that I didn't need to spend no damn money on another room. Golden sat her shoes down and went to the bathroom quickly. Pressing the pause button, I followed her into the bathroom. She was just staring into the mirror and she was pissed.

"What's the matter, babe?"

"Your sister is what's the matter, Yoshon. I could have gone to prison today." Tears poured down her face. I could tell that she had been holding them in for a minute and they were coming out because she was finally speaking.

"You good? What happened?" I reached over and touched her to make sure she was straight. What the fuck did Yolani do now?

"Babe, I don't want to start no problems, but your sister is a damn coke head. I was thinking we were going to some nice club, but she took us to the hood. After a drink, I was ready to go, but she had a friend she was supposed to meet. This man gave her some damn coke and not baggies. He gave her a big ass bubble ball of it packaged together." She stopped to take a break.

Yolani couldn't even take a break while being on vacation. She just had to work and the shit pissed me off. "Yolani is used to working. It don't matter where she's at; she's gonna work."

"No, that's not what the fuck she did. She opened the pack and started doing coke and drinking right in the club. When I told her I wanted to leave, she closed it up and tried to drive us home. I drove us back here, but we were pulled over, and she put the damn drugs in my purse. Talking about they wouldn't search me since I was a female. She's a fucking female too!" she yelled.

The jaw was tight as I thought about the shit that Yolani pulled tonight. Shit could have gone wrong and Golden had a son depending on her. Hearing that Yolani was doing drugs surprised me, but not too much. Her behavior had been different, and I chalked it up to her and Hazel going through shit. Never did I think she was out here doing fucking drugs. The shit had me pissed and I wanted to go over there and beat the shit out of Yolani like she was a nigga and not my sister.

"What happened?"

"I forgot to signal and they just let me go with a warning. Your sister was so high I had to get her to her suite before I could come here. I've never been in a situation like that and I feel like I'm about t—"

Her words were cut off as she rushed to the toilet and

vomited. I walked over and held her hair out of her face as she emptied her stomach. All I could smell was alcohol in the vomit she was spewing. When she was finished, she rinsed her mouth out and held onto the sink.

"You not pregnant or are you?" Shit, I had one on the way and as much as I would welcome one with Golden, right now wasn't the time for that.

"No, I always vomit when I'm scared or nervous. I wanted to do it in the car but didn't want to fuck up your car." She rinsed out her mouth. I could see her still shaking and it pissed me off that my sister put her in a situation like that.

"I'm sorry."

"Why? I'm not the kind of chick that blames others for someone's mistake. She did that, not you. I really wished I would have stayed home tonight." She walked over to me.

Wrapping my arms around her, I kissed her neck and sighed. "I'm going to talk to her tomorrow, I promise."

"Let's go to bed," she sighed. "I need to shower and I want to sleep," she told me.

"Bet. Go shower and I'll be waiting for you in the bed."

While Golden showered, I went to the kitchen to get some water out the fridge. Pit Pat was sitting on the counter and staring at me. "So, you finally know, huh?"

"Know what?"

"Yoshon, don't play dumb with me. Golden's hollering got me up and I heard everything. You finally know about your sister's little addiction."

"Why didn't you tell me?"

"Was trying to figure out how to. I had to process it first."

"She going to rehab or something. I'm not about to have her fucking running shit for me and she's a fucking crackhead."

"That's why Hazel eventually got fed up. I told her about it and she saw it for herself. I'm sure other things added to her leaving, but that had to be one of the reasons she just walked out on Yolani."

Leaning on the counter, "Golden could have gotten locked up. There's good cops, and then there's some bad ones too, but when I get pulled over, I'm not thinking of the good ones, I'm thinking of the ones who made the news for shooting an unarmed black man. Shit could have gone wrong for them tonight. The fuck was Yolani thinking?" That question was more to myself than it was to my grandmother.

"She wasn't thinking, baby. She hasn't been thinking for a long time. I know I was strict on y'all, especially Yolani, but I loved you both and tried to give y'all the best life I could."

"Stop trying to blame yourself for her mistakes. Yolani is doing what she's doing because she's fucking selfish and not thinking of her family. She thinks of herself before anyone else, and does what the fuck she wants. I'm going to talk to her tomorrow."

"I need to speak to both of you tomorrow. I think it's time for me to explain some things that I've been keeping quiet about."

Right now was the perfect time for me to tell her about the baby. Taking a deep breath, I opened my mouth. "I got a baby on the way."

"I know." was all she said and smiled. "I knew you would tell me when you ready to."

"How do you know?"

"I had forgot my keys to my car one afternoon and double backed in, and heard you on speakerphone in your office talking about it. I didn't say anything because I assumed you would tell me when you were ready."

"I'm sorry, Pit."

She stood up and walked over to me and hugged my stomach. "Don't be sorry, baby. This is your life and you needed to be confident in your decision before you told anybody. I'll love that baby just like I love you and your bull-headed sister; there's no doubt about that."

"Appreciate you." I kissed her on the forehead and she smiled.

"I also believe that Ms. Golden will be glad to step in and help. Y'all sleeping in the same bed now, so I see it's more than what you two knuckleheads are saying."

"It's more than that. We're taking it slow and haven't told Gyan. She doesn't want to tell him right away and I respect that."

"I do too. No need for that boy to be involved until you both are sure this is what you want to do," she smiled.

"I know this is what I want to do. She makes me feel different."

"I could tell. Go get some sleep and I'll talk to you in the morning." She rubbed my cheeks and went to her bedroom. Standing there, I wondered what she wanted to talk to me about. Pit Pat had a lot of secrets that she told us wasn't our business, but I knew my mind would be so focused on what she had to speak to us about.

When I went back into the bedroom, Golden was in the middle of the bed naked. Closing and locking the door behind me, I placed the water bottle down on the side table and crawled on the bed from the bottom of the bed. Spreading her legs, I made my way to her clit with my tongue leaking saliva because I couldn't wait to taste it. She had a rough night with Yolani, but I was trying to give her an early morning tongue lashing. Her body accepted me as I inserted my tongue into her peachy center. Lapping up her juices, she moaned and tossed her head back enjoying what I was doing to her below.

"Shon, what are you doing to me?" she moaned out and held my head as I slurped and licked her sticky center.

"Making you feel better, baby. With me, you ain't never going to bed angry," I said into her pussy and the vibration of my words caused her to arch her back.

Tonight, I didn't need no pussy. It was all about making her feel good and letting her bust her nut. She held onto my head as she fucked my face and I allowed her to. When I knew she was at her peak, she held onto my shoulders, and her body tensed up. I lapped her up caramel that oozed out of her special place. Coming up for air, I leaned over her and kissed her on the lips. She held me around the neck, and we shared a deep kiss as she wrapped her legs around me. I sucked on her neck as she kissed me on my face. Falling over on my side, I pulled her next to me, and we laid in the bed together.

"Why was I upset again?" she giggled and kissed me on the chest. "Why do you do this to me? You make me feel like I can rule the world, Yoshon Santana."

"Golden, you make me feel like I could take over the world and hand it to you, so you could rule it. Swear this shit feels so good that I never want it to end with us."

"And it doesn't have to end, baby. Long as you're honest with me and I'm honest with you, this can work. I have a lot of trust issues and hurt from the situation with Grand, and I'm working through it."

"Therapy," I mentioned.

"I don't want to go talk to some person who doesn't know me."

"Don't think of it that way. Think of it as a person who can see something that you may be missing. I went to therapy for a few years after I lost my mother. At first, I wasn't opened to the shit, but then it helped me. If Yolani went, I'm sure she wouldn't be battling the demons she's battling now."

"I'll think about it when we get back to New York."

"Nah, find one here and go. I'll fly them to New York whenever you have a session scheduled with them," I told her and I was serious. People underestimated mental health and that shit was real. Depression, anxiety and mental disorders were real shit and people overlooked them or called people crazy. I went through depression after Ashleigh passed away, so I knew the shit was real.

"It's not that serious."

"Nah, it is. I'll have my lawyers draw up those divorce papers too. Don't want that nigga having no claims to you."

She yawned. "Thank you, babe." She kissed me on the lips, and a few minutes later, I heard her snoring.

GOLDEN WAS up bright and early when I finally woke up and wiped the sleep out of my eyes. She was already showered and ready for the day. I watched as she walked around the room mumbling something to herself. She had on some short ass shorts that showed that big ass of hers. Golden couldn't hide her ass even if she tried. If the shorts wasn't enough, she had on a crop top that had the old school candy *Sugar Babies* logo on the shirt.

"Fuck you think you going with those little ass shorts?" I startled her. She turned around with a silly grin on her face.

"I thought you were sleep? I'm going to Lego land with Gyan today, and these aren't even short. You're just mad because my booty on display."

"Nah, go put on some sweats or something," I told her and she rolled her eyes. "I don't get an invite to Lego land? Damn."

"Me and Gyan are having mommy and son day. We're doing Universal and you're going so stop being a big baby. If you're good, I might bring you something back."

"Long as you and Gyan are back in one piece that's all I need you to bring me back." She walked over to me and kissed me on the lips.

"And we'll be back in one piece. About last night, don't go too hard on your sister." She touched my chest.

"Nah, that shit ain't nothing to play with. Today could have been a different scenario. I love you, Golden and that shit pissed me off." Did a nigga just tell her that I loved her? The shit came out my mouth so natural that I didn't even have to second guess it.

She leaned back and stared at me. "You serious? You love me?"

"I wouldn't have said it, if I didn't mean it." She grabbed my face with both of her hands and planted a kiss on my lips.

"I'm scared," she admitted. I could tell she was scared. That word scared the shit out of her, and it scared me too.

"Tell me why?"

"The last person that told me they loved me ended up hurting me in more than one way," she revealed.

"You think I'll hurt you?"

"Physically, no. Emotionally, you have the potential to. You have my heart in a lock, and that hasn't happened in a while, and I never thought that it would happen ever again."

"Just like I have the potential to hurt you emotionally, you have that same ability to do the same to me. Don't say it back, because I don't want you to say it because I said. Tell me when you're ready and on your time." I kissed her hands.

"Deal." She smiled and sealed our agreement with a kiss on the lips.

"Kissing, mom!" Gyan squealed when he entered the room. Golden's face turned to stone because she didn't want him to know about us.

"Gyan, what did I tell you about coming into rooms without announcing yourself?" she scolded him.

"Mom, can you leave the room so I can speak to Mr. Yoshon?" Gyan said as he placed his hands in the pockets of his shorts. I laughed because this boy had a personality that was out of this world.

"Boy, who d—"

"Ma, let him speak to me. He'll come get you when we're done."

Holding her arms up, she closed the door behind us. Gyan continued to walk toward me with his hands in his pockets. He did a little cough to clear his throat. "What are your intentions with my mommy? Don't tell her I used mommy either," he told me.

"I just want to love her and show her how a real man treats a woman."

"Are you going to hurt her like my dad did? I don't want to see my mommy crying and stuff like that again."

"Never. You got my word on that," I promised.

He smiled. "Okay, Mr. Yoshon, you can love on my mommy." He held his hand out and shook mine. "My mommy smiles more, and I found her singing and dancing like she used to do," he informed me.

"I want her to continue to smile; she deserves to smile."

"And we get to live in your big house too. So, can I get my room painted or something, that white wall is boring," he tried to add in some negotiations.

"Let me and your mama work that out, ight?"

"Okay. Time is money." He tapped his imaginary watch and I chuckled out loud.

"Oh, I know. I got you!"

He left the room and Golden returned with her Gucci bag slung over her shoulder. That girl wore that damn bag every-where she went. You didn't see her without that bag. "What did he have to say?"

"That's between me and him."

"Ugh, y'all both make me sick. I made you some lunch and it's in the kitchen. I'll see you later." She blew me a kiss.

"Ight. Bet. Be careful and call me when y'all get there."

"I will." She left out the room, and I got up, so I could go eat some food. My stomach was touching my damn back. It felt like

I went out for a damn night of drinking with how my stomach felt.

After brushing my teeth, showering and getting dressed, I emerged from my bedroom. Pit Pat had the patio door open, and she had food set out on the table with some water and lemonade. It was a beautiful day today and I now understood why Golden wanted to take Gyan out. She probably knew that Pit Pat wanted to talk to us, Pit Pat came out of her room and offered me a smile.

"Hey baby, I got some food on the patio and Yolani is on her way over."

"On her way over? She's across the hall."

"She went to run some errands this morning or something. Go out there and wait, and I hope your day is cleared," she told me.

I didn't have shit else planned for the day. All that I need Golden to handle with the dispensary was already handled. Today was a relaxing day, and I didn't want to get into some deep ass talk. Yolani had already fucked up half my day because soon as I woke up, I thought about the foul shit she did last night with Golden. Pit Pat had arranged for room service to bring different fruits, breakfast pastries, and eggs along with bacon. She had three types of orange juice and lemonades too. I sat down and rested my feet on the ottoman while I waited for Pit Pat and Yolani to get their shit together. Even if I didn't have shit to do today, the last thing I wanted to do was to be sitting here.

"What's good?" Yolani came strolling onto the patio with dark shades and an energy drink. She wore sweat shorts, wife beater and a pair of Gucci slides.

"Shit. You sure energy drinks good to be mixing with coke?"

She plopped down in the chair and didn't bother to remove her shades. "I fucked up last night. Golden held it down, so you know she'll ride for you." She tried to make it seem like that made it that much better. Not the fact that she fucking gave my girl her drugs to hold when the cops pulled them over.

"You just going to try and find some light in the fucked-up situation you created."

"Yeah. Bitches are expendable; we're not. Me getting booked in the system wasn't an option. You the one who taught me that." She nodded with a smirk on her face like she had done something good.

"Bitches, Yolani. Bitches! The women who carry themselves like sluts and want to do everything in the world to get my dick in their mouth, not her. Golden isn't one of those bitches."

"Shit, if Hazel was there, I would have done the same. Hell, I've done it a few times when we went out to dinner. While she in the bathroom, I slip it in her purse and slip it out before we make it back to the crib."

Who created this monster? Was I responsible for doing this shit? I handed Yolani an empire where she didn't need to put nearly as much work as I did. She got the luxury of bossing niggas around, and they listened because they knew it would be hell to pay from me. Anything she wanted, I made sure to work ten times as hard to provide it for her. How did I go wrong? They said you couldn't have a conscious and be in the streets. That was something I had a hard time doing. I couldn't look away from the foul shit that went on in the streets. For every person I had to murk, there was an anonymous donor who donated money for the funeral. The streets wasn't for me. You couldn't have a heart and deal with the streets, and my sister had learned and adapted something I never wanted for her. If it was one thing, I wanted her to have it was compassion. I wanted her to rule the streets, but also have a heart. It was clear that Yolani didn't have a damn heart. If she did, she wouldn't be sitting here and telling me that she slips coke into her wife's purse occasionally.

"Yo, I can't sit here and listen to this shit," I sat my English muffin down on the coffee table. "The fuck is up with you?"

"This been me. You gotta do people dirty before they get a

chance to do you dirty," she replied. "You need to stop acting like you didn't teach me some of this."

"Nah, in the streets all bets are off. You gotta get a nigga before he do you wrong, but you're sitting here talking about your fucking wife!" I roared.

"That bitch in her feelings and then some." She leaned back and relaxed like she wasn't talking about Hazel. Hazel wasn't even my shorty and I was pissed like she was.

Hazel deserved more than what the fuck Yolani was sitting up here giving her. Despite what they were going through in their relationship, she had always been there for Yolani when it counted the most. She was sitting up here talking like she was some bitch in the street, instead of the woman she claimed she loved.

"You only care are about your fucking self. Nobody else fucking matters, right? Like you putting coke in Golden's purse."

"She was good. I would have bailed her out. Only because she's your little plaything. If she wasn't, I'd be on a flight back to New York."

"Shut the f—"

"Aye, I don't want to hear that cutting up. Sit down and calm down, Yoshon," Pit Pat finally graced us with her presence. If I sat out here with this ruthless bitch for one minute, I couldn't promise what would happen to her. Yolani had me so fucked up with the shit that continued to spill out of her mouth.

"What's up? I gotta go and handle some shit before I get on a flight back home. This trip was a fucking waste," Yolani openly cursed in front of our grandmother. I slipped once in and a while, but I made sure not to do it when I was speaking to her.

"What's up?" Pit Pat mocked.

"I mean, you said you gotta talk to us... I wanna know what's going on?" she smartly replied like she wasn't talking to the woman that raised us.

"Yolani, I will put you over my knee an—"

"Pit, I'm a little too old and fast for you to be putting me over your shoulder. For real, what's going on?"

"Then damn drugs. When you started doing those, Yolani?"

"Why both of y'all so concerned with what the fuck I do? If I do a little coke to destress, what is it to y'all?"

"Because then you become the crack head of the family with the thinning hair." Pit stood there with her hand on her hips. "I want this shit to stop now. You don't need to be doing drugs, Yolani. If this...." she allowed her voice to trail off and sat down.

"If what?" I spoke up.

"It's about time I told y'all about the business. I've been hiding for years, and Baru has hated what I've done. Told me I spoil and baby you both and you need to know."

Sitting up, she had me worried. What the fuck was she talking about and what does Baru, my supplier, have to do with this? "What you talking about, Pit?"

"Yoshon, do you think my brother magically made a trip here on your 18th birthday? Do you think I chose to live in Belize?

"Pit, what's up with all these weird ass questions? And who the hell is your brother?" She had me more confused than I originally was.

"Baru is my half-brother and he's your uncle. The family business is guns," she revealed and I leaned back in the chair.

"You mean to tell me that we own a fucking factory of guns and we've been buying them? Yo, I'm really about to take over the streets."

"Shut your fucking mouth!" Pit Pat raised her voice louder than we had ever heard. She was so loud that even I shut up and I wasn't even speaking. "You will not speak a word of what I'm telling you. If you do, I can't help what happens to you."

"Your Santana name means a lot to you because you felt like you built. It's been built long before we knew about you, baby boy," she chuckled.

"I'm lost." Yolani slapped her forehead.

"The Santana Cartel is one of the most ruthless cartels in Belize. We have family members all over the world and they meet once a month to discuss operations in the cartel. Your uncle Baru is the head of the cartel since his father's father was the man who started it. We're siblings by the same father, not mother. He couldn't step down until a boy was born. Yes, you have plenty of male cousins, but they weren't my papa's grandchildren. Your mother is my only child, and she can't take lead of the cartel since she's a woman."

"What the fuck? So, I can't take lead of the fucking cartel because I gotta pussy and not a dick?"

"You would never be head of the cartel for reasons that have nothing to do with your genitals."

"Why didn't you never tell us this?" Why did she hold all of this from us? If she didn't tell Yolani, I would understand. But, me? Why did she hold this from me? Yolani was too much of a hothead and wouldn't be able to process it the way it needed to. Even Baru lied to me. This man was a mentor to me and this entire time he was of kin to me. This shit was too wild for me and I had to lean even further in the seat.

"Baby, I wanted to tell you, and something stopped. I know what the Santana cartel is about and I know how ruthless they are. I figured what you do in America was enough and you didn't need to get involved. Baru is ready to step down. The man is in his seventies and he's ready to retire with his twenty-five-year-old wife. He's been on my neck to tell you or he would tell you."

"Yo, this shit is wild."

"I still find Baru's fine ass wife and his old ass disgusting."

"Shut the fuck up!" I barked at my sister. Here our grandmother was sitting here and telling us that we had ties to a cartel, and she was worried about what our uncle and his wife looked like. The shit pissed me off because I was trying to process this shit.

"I came here on a student visa and I was eight months pregnant. The women in our family don't carry too big, so I was able to disguise it well. Not even Baru knew until I got to the states. I took a few classes because that's what Papa wanted me to do. When I had your mother, it was the best day of my life. It was sunny, she slipped right on out, and I got to leave a few hours after. Papa wasn't pleased because she wasn't a boy, but he loved his granddaughter with all his heart," she spoke from the heart. I could tell from the way she stared off into space as she spoke. "When your mother turned eighteen, she met some boy. I thought it was a silly crush and it would fade away. When she came in the house with a sonogram, I knew it wasn't a silly crush anymore. When I told Baru and my papa, they were excited. This was a chance at them having the baby boy they've been waiting for. When we found out you were a boy, the whole town where we are from celebrated. Baru got the call at three in the morning that you were born, and you were to be named Yoshon Dadir Baru Santana."

I finally knew where the fuck my damn name came from. All my life I wondered where my long ass name came from and my grandmother played it off like it was my mother's doing.

"Man, this shit is crazy. How does Baru know that I want to be a part of the cartel?"

"This is why I hid it. You're not given a choice; this is your life. You're meant to stand head of the cartel."

"I'm not moving to no damn Belize. You live in the slums and shit, for what?"

"Buoy!" she hollered in her accent. It only came out when she was passionate about what she was speaking about. "I don't live in the slums. We have a family compound that looks over all of Belize and the coasts."

"All this celebration for this nigga, what about me?"

"Your father named you. Baru had a man that he wanted you to marry when you were eighteen. He's a prominent member of the cartel, but I told him about your situation."

"That I'd rather lick pussy than get my pussy fucked?"

Pit Pat was disgusted by Yolani's actions. I could tell from the way she kept cutting her eyes at her. "Your mother was supposed to kill your father. He was stealing, and since she brought him in, she had to take him out. Some way he found out and decided to beat her to the punch and murder her. I never forgave myself for that. Baru put so much pressure on her to handle him and I knew she wasn't ready. Your mother didn't want this life and it was pushed upon her. I didn't want that for you both."

"That's why that nigga got dealt with."

"Sorry to burst your bubble, baby girl. Your father was already handled before you got there. All you did was added bullets to his body. The bottle of gin he was consuming had poison in it already. He was dying, either way, all you did was expedite it."

"Why did mommy struggle? She worked hard as hell and sometimes two or three jobs at a time."

"Your mother didn't struggle. You both had a nice roof over your head, no? Anything you wanted your mother provided for you."

"She did," I agreed. I guess I thought I should have been living in mansions being that I was heir to the throne of the Santana Cartel.

"Yeah, but we went to public school," Yolani's dumb ass had to blurt out.

"Oh, so you had a bad life because you went to public school? That was your mother's choice. All of it was her choice. Her fear was raising entitled and soft children, which she didn't."

"Where do we go from here?"

She sighed. "We take a trip back home so the family can meet you. They know about you all, but besides Baru, they have never met you both. If you could pull your nose out of cocaine long enough, I would like you to be there," she shot at Yolani.

"Funny," she chuckled.

"This is too much for me to take in at once. I need to take a nap and think about this alone." I stood up and walked over to my grandmother. Tears fell down her cheeks. I knew this was a hard conversation to have.

"I never wanted to lie to you about this."

"You were protecting us. Mama left, and there was no one protecting us, so you stepped up and did that. I don't fault you for that at all, Grandma."

She looked at me and stood up. Wrapping her arms around me, she sniffled into my stomach. "I love you both so much. This isn't the life I would have chosen for neither of you."

"Stop stressing. I don't want your pressure getting back up," I warned her and kissed her forehead. "Know what I'm craving?"

"Some Johnny cakes." I smiled, knowing that would make her feel better. Catering and caring for us was something that brought her so much peace. After the afternoon we had, she needed something to take her mind off all we discussed today.

"I can get to the store and get some ingredients to make them," she smiled and cheered up. "I'll go make a list and have Golden take me when she gets back."

"Okay." I kissed her once more. Walking past Yolani pissed me the fuck off. "Me and you will talk at another time."

"Yeah, ight. Sound like this nigga 'bout to become the king of Wakanda," she laughed at her own joke. Even Pit Pat followed behind me and left her dumb ass on the patio. Right now, I needed a nap and to rest my mind.

Me, being the head of a cartel. I was born and raised to be the head of this cartel. It was in the cards for me since I've been in the womb. I couldn't let my grandmother down, and I had to step up and do what I needed to do, even if my heart told me that I didn't want to do it. Running my businesses and finding love was all on my list. Then, I had to think of my daughter. She was being born into a life I didn't want for her. Yashleigh was to go to college and become a lawyer, doctor or whatever the hell she wanted to become, not be the heiress to a throne. Even though women weren't allowed, I'd be damn if my daughter didn't sit on the same throne as her father. Besides, Pit and Baru would be buried and gone by then. I got comfortable in the bed and closed my eyes. At once, all my thoughts consumed my mind, and I sorted them from the comforts of my bed.

10

Golden

"MOM, can I please go and play the game?" Gyan asked soon as we got out of the town car from Lego Land. It wasn't enough he had me pay over a hundred dollars for some small Lego figurine, but he just had to play the game tonight too.

"I thought we were hanging tonight?" My feelings were hurt that he would rather go and play that stupid game than hang with me.

We spent the entire day together and had some many pictures and laughs. It was one of those memories he would remember forever. Hell, I know I would. If I never saw another Lego in my life, I would be good. Being around hyper kids all day had me tired, and I just wanted some wine and a bubble bath. For the entire day, I didn't think about the situation that happened with Yolani the night before. The more I thought about it, the more I got upset all over again. How could she set me up like that? What I thought would be a nice night out with Yoshon's sister turned into me being on an episode of Power. It wasn't like I was stupid and didn't know what Yoshon did. He kept that away from me and I respected him for it. He didn't include me in it, and I never heard him talking about it either. Grand was the opposite. I could walk in the house from a long day, and he would have coke scattered all over the kitchen table.

Gyan still had perfect memory of that, and I had to tell him it was baby powder and daddy was bottling it up, so we could have some in the closet. He believed me and never spoke about it again, but every once in a while, he would reminisce and ask me about it like my answer would change. Of course, when he was older, he would know that the baby powder was in fact coke. Yolani didn't know me like that to pull some shit like that. Then when I yelled at her, she chuckled like the shit was funny, and she did this shit for fun. I didn't want to see or speak to her ass because if I did, I might punch her in the face. The shit she pulled was something I couldn't forget nor forgive. My son was my entire world and the thought of me being snatched away from him scared the shit out of me. With the amount of coke she had on her, I could have easily been booked for trying to distribute it. While she thought this was funny, this was my life.

"We're back!" I sang as we walked through the double doors of our suite. It was quiet and I didn't hear anything.

"I knew I heard some yelling." Pit Pat came from her room. Her eyes were red as if she had been crying.

"You alright?" I mouthed, and she nodded her head with a weak smile forced upon her lips. She reached down and ruffled Gyan's hair.

"How was the amusement park, boy?"

"It was fun. I wished you could have been there." He hugged her around her waist. Gyan wasn't that much shorter than Pit Pat.

I loved their bond. Gyan had one grandmother that was alive, and she didn't reach out too much. He had never got to experience how it was having a grandmother. I had been blessed to be raised by my grandmother, and I took that for advantage. Pit Pat wasn't his grandmother, yet she acted like she was, and Gyan respected her as if she was his grandmother.

"I'm too old to be out there running like a 'youngin. Long as you had fun, that's all that matters."

"I did."

"Okay. Go ahead and get a bath ran and come eat when you're done." She kissed the top of his head and he ran off to their room.

Pit Pat's slippers shuffled to the kitchen and she went to warm up the food room service must have brought while we were gone. "Are you alright? You're always there for me, and I just want to be there for you."

"My granddaughter is addicted to drugs and her brother hates her. I didn't raise these two like this." She heated up the chicken with the rice.

"Yoshon could never hate his sister, no matter how hard he tried. He's upset with her and just wants her to do right. Pit, you did good with the both of them. I don't know Lani too much, but she just needs to find he—"

"Keep it like what you said. You don't fucking know me," Yolani's raspy voice sounded from behind me. "You fucking my brother, so you think you can speak on me? Nah." She walked into the kitchen.

"Lani, watch your mouth," Pit Pat sternly warned her.

"You sitting here and letting her run her mouth about me. She don't know shit about me and never will. I'm just meeting you and you trying to form your opinions about me."

"You're right. I don't know you, and with the route, you're going I don't want to know you."

"Bitch, if I allowed you, you would be trying to get with me."

"I like ribeye, not fish," I replied and stepped back. She was getting to close for comfort and I eyed the knife. If I had to, I would stick this shit right into her damn eye.

"Yeah, you fronting. The fuck you using my brother for? Do

you even love the nigga? Yoshon always had a thing for women in need. Ashleigh was in need, and now your homeless ass," Her words cut me like a damn knife, still, I didn't drop one tear.

"Alright now. Get the hell out of this suite!" Pit Pat hollered. "After all we spoke about today, and you're sitting up in my damn face, high as ever. Get the hell on!" she hollered even louder than the first.

"Don't worry about it. I'll leave." I touched Pit Pat's arm and left the suite. I wanted to; no, I needed to leave. If I didn't, I was going to hurt Yolani's feelings horribly. She was upset with the way her life was going so she wanted to hurt someone. It wasn't that I was with her brother, she wanted what her brother had. Yoshon had been blessed to find two women who cared for him immensely.

He didn't have to act like something he wasn't. Yoshon was rough and would fuck a nigga up in a heartbeat, still, he was soft and had a sensitive side to him. He moved his way and to the beat of his own drum. I loved that he didn't give a fuck how he looked to people. He showed he had feelings and emotions and didn't try to hide them. In fact, he made me upset because he always wanted to talk about them. With all his feelings and emotions, it didn't take away that he was a thug. Yolani was trying to be this heartless thug and it wasn't working out for her. Hazel wasn't with her when she arrived, and she spent the entire night at the club talking about how many bitches she fucked. Yolani was so focused on quantity and not quality. She would rather have seven bad bitches, instead of one real woman that could probably change her entire life.

"Where you heading?" I heard Yoshon's voice behind me. He had to be in the room sleep because his voice was always the deepest when he woke up.

"To go clear my mind. Your sister is tripping for real."

"I'll come with you," he told me and walked beside me. I didn't want him to feel like he had to choose between me or his sister. In the end, we were both grown, and he didn't need to choose anyone of us. Yoshon could have relationships with the both of us.

"You were sleep?"

"Yeah. Pit talked about some shit today and I needed a minute to collect my thoughts without actually thinking about them."

"Want to talk about it?"

"Nah. Not yet. Wanna talk about something?"

"Your sister is a piece of work." I shook my head. "What is wrong with her?"

"She's so busy trying to be a Brownsville Bully, that she's not realizing that she's pushing her family away. I told her if she wanted to keep fucking with that shit, she could stay the fuck away from me. Pit Pat is always going to check up on her, but I'm not doing that shit with her. As far as she's concerned, she can go start her own shit."

"How do you sleep at night, babe?"

"What you mean?"

"You supply drugs and guns into the community. You're a good man, love God, and you take care of your family. Why do you do this?"

"This is the family's business," he sighed. "You think I feel good about the shit I do? The shit fucks with me every day. Each time I open a newspaper or look at the news, I hear about a gun I know I supplied that took the life of another person."

"Paying for funerals and helping families isn't going to clear your guilty conscious," I reminded him. "Do you want your daughter to know that her father is the man behind all the killings in the hood?"

"Goldie, if they don't get it from me, they gonna get it from someone else."

"So? That's that man's karma, not yours. You own so many businesses, Yoshon. You don't need to be doing this anymore, so why are you?"

"Because it's the family's business. I was born into this shit, and even if I wanted to leave it all at the table, I can't," he revealed.

"You can. You have a choice."

"Nah. You have a choice. Some people don't have choices and have to do what their family wants. I have the choice to help out the communities that I destroy, or help out the families with financial shit. Stepping away? I don't have that choice."

I wasn't understanding what he meant by he didn't have the option of stepping away. Last I checked, this was a free country, and everyone had the right to say no to something. From his body language, I could tell he didn't want to speak any further on this subject. Long as he knew how I felt about it, that's all that mattered. I wasn't telling him what he should do, but I was reminding him that he could pay for a million funerals and help the whole community out. Still, he was the same man that was destroying the community. It didn't matter that he tried to help his mental by appointing his heartless sister to handle operations. At the end of the day, he was the puppet master pulling the strings. He could cut the strings and go on to live a good life if he wanted.

"You know I'm here for you if you need anything. Even though I'm homeless," I giggled to lighten the mood.

What Yolani said to me hurt my feelings and made me feel a way, but I wasn't going to allow her to hurt me. I was a good person, and I was down on my luck now, but that wouldn't be forever. She was someone that was hurt and taking it out on everybody. What she needed was to go to church and seek the Lord to get her through whatever demons she was currently battling. Pit Pat was beating herself up and thinking this was somehow her fault and it wasn't. She did all she could as a grandmother and this was something that Yolani was battling. She was the only person that could help herself in the end. If she needed someone to talk to, despite all the foul shit she said to me; I would be there without a doubt. Everyone deserved the option to change, and if she wanted to change, then I would be open to having a relationship with her. If she didn't, then she could stay as far away from me, because I would beat her ass.

"I know and I appreciate you for that." He swooped me in a hug and kissed me on top of my head. This just felt right. Any time he touched, kissed or hugged me, everything felt like this was what was supposed to happen. For once, I had gotten it right with a man, and I didn't want anything to go wrong. I glanced down at my phone and sighed when I saw Grand's number. Ignoring the call, I slipped my phone back into my pocket and continued to walk alongside Yoshon.

11

Hazel

$\mathcal{L}$ *as Vegas, Nevada*

SHAKING, I stared at the six-carat ring that was on my finger along with the wedding band. It was a little loose, but it was the best he could do on such last-minute terms. We stood in front of his two brothers and said, 'I do.' I cried a few times because my parents or Mo weren't there, but I was married. Denim had his lawyer fly out to get the papers, so he could file them for real. I was so nervous about being someone's wife. We didn't talk about finances, all we did was jump right into it. When you know, you know, and I knew I wanted to be with Denim. I was just too scared to take a leap so far. What if it didn't work out? What if he did me the same way that Yolani did? It was things like that, that constantly consumed my thoughts. Then, I thought about his child I was carrying and how loving he was toward me, and it all went away.

"How you feeling, Mrs. Debix?" He smirked and squeezed my hand as walked into a restaurant. We were meeting his lawyer and his wife for dinner.

"I feel like someone isn't going to pinch me from this dream any minute." I couldn't wipe the smile off my face even if I tried to.

Denim snatched me to the side and hemmed me up against the glass of the restaurant and kissed me on the lips. "Then you better get used to this every damn day." He kissed me on the lips and I accepted it.

"Do you think we did the right thing by not including our parents? I'm worried about what my parents will think, and your mother too."

"Babe, stop worrying about all of the stuff that don't matter. We did it the way we wanted to, and they'll have to get out of their feelings. We don't need to be worried about that; we're on a honeymoon."

"Eventually, we'll have to worry about that, Dem. What about where we'll live?" All this stuff that didn't bother me the entire flight here was all coming up at once, and I was panicking.

"You'll move into my apartment. It's two bedrooms and enough for all three of us. When Tailor comes to visit, she can share a room with her brother."

"Brother, huh? You just know you're getting your boy this time."

"God wouldn't surround me with so many women," he chuckled and kissed me on the nose. "Boy or girl, I'm satisfied."

"Look at you two lovebirds. Can't even make it into the restaurant. I just overnighted your papers to my assistant and look at 'yous." His Italian lawyer walked up with his wife on his arm. She was a beautiful, mocha colored woman. I didn't take his lawyer for being married to a black woman.

"Congratulations, you two. I love, love," she smiled and hugged both me and Denim. "And thank you for the free trip. Dinner is on us, and I refuse for you to state otherwise." She pecked him on the cheek and giggled.

We all walked into the restaurant and was seated immediately. Denim held my chair out and pushed me in, just like Lucci did for his wife. I stared down at my ring again and couldn't believe I had married Denim. When I said it in his apartment, it felt so right. I couldn't lose him. Denim meant a lot to me, and by me playing games, I almost lost him for good.

"How are you loving the Venetian?" she asked me about the hotel.

"I've never stayed here. It's so beautiful."

"We live in California so it isn't a long flight. Me and Lucci get away from the kids twice a week and lay low here," she smiled.

"Kids? How old and how many?"

"We have two sets of twins. Our boys are six, and our daughter and son are four."

"House full, huh? I see why you're getting away."

"Yes, it's important to have time for mommy and daddy." She accepted the flute of champagne from her husband. "Do you have any kids?"

"I'm carrying one now," I smiled. For the first time, I felt so proud and excited to announce that I was pregnant. Then, to be pregnant by the man I married today was everything and more.

"Well, you're going to have to head to California when it's time to do the nursery. I have a beautiful boutique that has the best upscale baby furniture, and you need to let us furnish your nursery," she boasted about her company. With the way she bragged about getting away with her husband, I didn't think she had a business.

"I'll be sure to give you a call when it's time for that." I smiled.

When she said the word upscale, I knew it wasn't a store I was going to be shopping in. This child was going to know a budget.

Just because my shop made good money didn't mean that I was going to be buying expensive things. His parents owned businesses, so that meant one month we could be up and the next, we could be down. I refused to raise my child thinking that the luxurious life was a life he was going to live. Now, he would get things and nine times out of ten, I would spoil him, but paying over five thousand dollars for a baby crib and some chester was outrageous.

"How's business been in New York?" Lucci questioned Denim.

"Man, it's been booming. I don't want to count my eggs yet, but in a year, I'll probably be opening another store. This store gets crazy traffic and I had to hire three security guards."

"Amazing. When you pitched this idea years ago, I knew it would be brilliant. The store on the west coast has been doing amazing too. I drive past there on my way to the office and it's busy as usual. What's next? A baby, a wife... man, you are blessed."

"I am. I'm just gonna get used to being someone's husband and get ready for this baby. Tailor is going to be here soon to visit. Her mother is going out of town with her boyfriend."

"Oh, you allow her to have a boyfriend?" he laughed, and I didn't know what he meant by that. What did he mean that Denim *allowed* her to have a boyfriend? Last I checked, she was grown and they had a co-parenting relationship.

"Man, it wasn't something I wanted. She claims she in love and she's tired of being lonely," he downplayed it.

"How do you think she's going to take it that you told her she couldn't have a boyfriend and you have a whole life?" he laughed.

"She gonna have to deal with it. Hazel is my wife and she's not going anywhere." He lifted my hand and placed a kiss on it.

It was this that I loved about this man. I didn't need to fight for my place in his life. He constantly reminded me and had no problem telling anyone who wanted to know that I was his woman. He was telling people I was his woman before I was even his woman. It felt nice to be claimed, appreciated and loved. Being with Yolani and then Denim was night and day. They were two different people and did things totally different. It was going to take me a while to get used to how Denim did things. To him, I was his queen, and there wasn't anything he wouldn't do for me. If this nigga thanked me one more time for keeping the baby, I was going to chokeslam his ass. Keeping the baby wasn't about him, it was more about me and what I wanted. All I've been doing was begging Yolani about us having a baby. She never wanted to hear me and would laugh it off. Now that I was blessed with a baby, why was I trying to get rid of it? God was only giving me what I had been asking for, and I wouldn't dear deny a blessing from the man above.

We had an amazing dinner with Lucci and his wife. Me and Denim walked through the hotel holding hands and smiling like newlyweds.

"Baby, one second, let me answer this call, it's my business partner," Denim told me and walked off to answer his phone. Usually, I would be jealous and suspicious of someone stepping away to answer a call, but not this time. I knew that Denim was being truthful when he told me that he was handling business. I smiled because I thought about the first time he called me. He happened to have called me on my business phone, which caused me to giggle.

Yeah?" I answered my business phone. It distracted me from the rage I felt about Yolani's ass not bringing her ass home.

"Why you gotta answer the phone like that?" Denim laughed over the line. My heart skipped a beat when I heard his voice.

"Denim? How did you get my number?" I gasped and sat up in my bed. It was amazing how I was angry moments before, and now my mood had altered almost instantly.

"I mean, you changed your number when you got with ol' girl... the only way I could let you know I'm back in town was from the number on your shop."

"How do yo—"

"You know my mama was gonna put me on," he cut me off and I laughed.

"So, how are you? How long are you back in town?" Each question spilled out the mouth as fast as the first one was asked.

"I'm back for good. Just opened a sneaker store up in Harlem," he informed me. *"Found me a nice ass condo over in Bayridge, Brooklyn."*

My heart dropped when he said he was back in New York for good. *"W...what made you leave Los Angeles?"*

"The shop I opened there is doing good, and it was time to open one in my hometown, feel me?"

"Uh huh... so what's up?"

"Meet me for dinner tonight."

"Tonight? It's snowing outside."

"Snow ain't never hurt nobody... I'm sending a car to come scoop you," he told me and ended the call.

How did he know where I lived? Denim was the one who got away. He was my ex-boyfriend, and we dated for a few months before he moved to California. Denim wanted me to move with him and I declined. It was around the same time that Yolani had told me she loved me. How was I supposed to up and move with her revealing that to me? I couldn't and that's why I told Denim that I couldn't move with him. He didn't get mad or shit on me, he told me that he would always keep in contact with me, and he did. Except, now I was married to Yolani. I couldn't just pick up where we left off when I had a wife.

"The fuck you clutching your phone to your chest for?" Yolani's raspy voice made me jump out of my skin.

Putting my phone back on the nightstand, I recovered quickly. *"My phone should be the least of your fucking worries. Where the fuck you been all night?"*

"In my damn car. Shit was too damn deep and coming down too bad to keep driving. My phone died too, so you know I was bored as fuck." Yolani messed with her hair when she lied. Right now, she was messing with the tip of one of her four braids.

"Why the fuck do you feel the need to lie to me? You weren't in your car the entire night, Yolani, so why you lying?"

"Damn baby, I was calling you." Denim broke me from my flashback I was having. Thinking back to the arguments we used to have didn't make me miss Yolani's selfish ass. It did make me wonder how she was doing, and if she was alright. You didn't just stop caring for people overnight. Even if she wasn't with me, I still wanted the best for her. With her doing coke and thinking that it was fine to do it, I worried about her a lot.

Leaving her was something that I had to do for myself. I would have gotten sucked into a web that I'm not sure I would be able to get myself out of. I loved Pit Pat and Yoshon, but I couldn't stay in a toxic relationship because my love I had for them. Knowing them, I knew they would be happy for me. I made a mental note to give Pit Pat a call when I made it back to the hotel room.

"Sorry, I was zoned out," I smiled.

"Remember tonight is the night for my friend's party. We going to a club and then some strip club."

"I remember. I'm going upstairs to lay down and watch movies. Today was eventful and I just want to order room service."

"We just ate," he laughed.

"Um, that little itty-bitty food. I'll be hungry right again. Plus, this baby makes me hungry."

"That baby is the size of a pea, stop fronting," he called my greedy ass out. I knew the baby wasn't making me eat all of this, but I was hungry as hell and needed someone to blame.

"Shut the hell up!" I pushed him as we stepped onto the elevator.

"I'm just saying. You out here 'bout to be all swollen with my baby in your stomach and my ring on your finger." He smirked as he said those words.

"Who would have thought? I didn't see my day ending with me being your wife. It's funny how life works."

"Yeah, the man upstairs is funny with the shit he does."

"Um, did you just curse with God in the same sentence?"

"My bad." He pulled my hand and we exited the elevator. For some reason, Pit Pat was on my mind, and I needed to call and have a conversation with her. If I was home, I would drive to the house and be with her. Just sitting near that woman has calmed down and made me feel at peace. Yolani took her grandmother for granted and liked to call her annoying and never appreciated her. This was a woman that dedicated her entire life to her grand-kids after her daughter passed away.

"Go and shower so you're not late. I don't want them blaming your new wife on your being late."

"Damn, that was my excuse," he shot back and I flipped the middle finger at him. "I'm fucking with you. Your ass better stay up and wait for me tonight."

"Bring home some Henny dick and I'll be ready," I winked.

When a nigga had Henny dick, it was the best dick in the world. They never got tired and could go for hours. Having a plastic dick being rammed in your hole for years, and then finally getting the real thing had me addicted. While women loved to complain about Henny dick, I was one that welcomed it with open arms. The way me and Denim went at it, I don't know why I was shocked to find out that I was pregnant with his baby. Sex was just another thing that we were on the same level with. Often, you had a person who you could talk with and connect with. Then, when it came to having sex, the connection was only there mentally and not physically. When it came to the both of us, we got it on both mentally and physically.

I scrolled through my phone and found Pit Pat's number. While Denim was in the shower, I dialed her number and waited for her to answer. "Hello. Hazel, are you okay?"

"I'm fine, Pit. You were just on my mind and I wanted to call and check on you."

"I'm fine," she sighed and I could tell I had woke her up. "I'm worried about you. How are you? Yolani won't talk much about you."

"That's fine. We're broken up. I'll let her tell you why."

"You don't think that you will get back together? Hazel, you know you're like another granddaughter to me."

"Pit, I got married to my ex-boyfriend. I need time to tell Yolani; I just wanted you to know why I haven't been around."

"Married? Lawd, how when you're a Santana?"

"Yolani never filed the papers so we're not legally married." I guess Yolani never felt that she had to explain this to her grandmother. Then again, I wasn't surprised. She never told her grandmother anything.

"I pray for my bull-headed granddaughter of mine. I love you, Hazel and you need to come see me when I get back to New York."

"I will."

"Nothing changes between us. I want to meet that husband of yours," she surprised me when she said that.

"You will. Go back to sleep and I love you."

"I love you too, baby." I smiled as I ended the call and undressed from the white silk sundress I wore.

Laying down, I shed a tear. Just talking to Pit Pat had me emotional. I loved that woman. She accepted me with open arms and had always been there for me. She was there for me more than my own mother was. Eventually, I got tired of thinking and drifted off to sleep.

12

Alicia

"WHY ARE you even having communication with your ex-wife in the first place?" I held the phone in my hand.

Grand rolled over and grilled me as I stood with his cell phone in my hand. While I was cleaning our bedroom, I ran across his phone on the dresser. The shit pissed me off when I noticed he had been stalking his ex-wife's Facebook page and had sent her a message along with a phone call. I knew all about Golden and how she cheated on him and ran off with his son. That bitch didn't realize how great of a man she had, and that was why I was sitting in her place. Grand was a hard-working man who loved and appreciated his family, and she couldn't handle that. There was no need for him to have no contact with her stupid ass. Each time he brought her up and how she did him wrong, it pissed me off. If cheating and leaving wasn't enough, she lied to the police about him raping her and Grand was arrested. If I ever saw her in life, I promised myself that I was going to whip her ass all up and through the street.

"Why the fuck you going through my phone?" was the first question that he wanted to ask instead of answering my damn question.

"Grand, don't play with me right now. After all she done to you; you writing her. You lucky I'm carrying your baby, because I would beat her ass."

"Chill. You forgot I got a seed with her? All of this is for my son. I gotta play nice to see my son," he explained and I calmed down. "I'm doing all the watching of her social media because I want to make sure my son is straight and being take care of," he continued to make me feel at ease.

"Babe, we need to just get custody of him. When she skipped town with him, you should have done that."

"With my record and just being released, my lawyer advised me that I shouldn't be thinking about that right. All I'm trying to do is get money, chill and love on you, baby." He held his arms out, and I climbed into bed into his arms.

"I know. She just makes me so mad because of what she did to you. You didn't deserve that." I didn't understand why Grand took it so lightly. I went more hard for him about the situation and he's the one who actually went through it.

"Stop stressing my baby out about something neither of us can change. I told you about going through my phone too." He pinched my cheeks and I giggled.

"Sorry, you know these bitches get me crazy. How many bitches back in Virginia was mad that a New York girl snagged you up."

"Yeah, they were in their feelings," he confirmed what I had already knew.

I met Grand when I was heading to have fun with my girls. Never did I think I was going to find love after hooking up with this man. He beat my pussy up so good that he had me stuttering on my way back to my hotel. That next night I tried avoiding him and he found me and snagged me up. This dude had a way with words and was so different than his dumb ass friends. After that weekend, I left with his number and the promise that I would come back alone to kick it with him. Three weeks later, my ass was riding the bus down to see him. He showed me around his stomping grounds and then showed me his crib. This house was beautiful with all the bells and whistles. When we were just flirting on at Virginia Beach, I thought he was broke like his friends. I mean, they had money, but they were acting broke like they couldn't buy my girls a drink.

It was then that I had landed what I've been looking for my entire life. Someone to take care of me. Grand took me and upgraded my life instantly. I could thank my ill nana because he was hooked. When I first was visiting him, I came down on the bus. Once he started taking care of me, I was taking Uber rides from Brooklyn all the way to Virginia. He footed the entire bill and didn't even trip about tipping the driver. Eventually, he hired the driver to do the drives off the books. He slowly opened up about things and we grew closer to each other. When I found out that I was pregnant, I knew I had to tell my aunt and uncle and bring him, so he could meet them. Grand knew I didn't want to live in Virginia, so he got a condo, so I could stop sleeping on my friend's couch.

My aunt was always happy for any and everything I did. She was my biggest cheerleader since my parents died. My cousin, Hazel, she was always skeptical and had smart remarks about my multiple relationships. Nothing I did was ever good enough for my big cousin. The more I tried to make her proud, the less she seemed like she liked me. Living with Hazel was hell. She was spoiled and liked things her way. I was always the annoying little cousin, even though we were a year apart. Soon as I was able to, I got my shit and moved out with a boyfriend I was seeing at the time. My aunt begged me to stay and wanted me to be here until I found an apartment. Living with my moody cousin wasn't an option for me.

The thing about it, was that I didn't hate my cousin. I looked up to her in so many ways. She was much smarter, stronger and business savvy than I was. Her obsession had been nails since I could remember, and she would do nails out the basement for less than she was worth. When she opened her shop, I was so proud of her. As we got older, we both had things going with our own lives that we didn't connect much. Once in a while, I called to check in on her, and she did the same for me. Now that we were both pregnant, I was hoping we could bond and become closer. We were both about to embark on motherhood and didn't know what to expect, so we could lean on each other for support. That was my hope, and I prayed my cousin had the same mindset as I did. Majority of her issues with me came from her own issues with her mother. My aunt wasn't the biggest fan of anything that Hazel did. She didn't like that she did nails, she didn't like that she liked women, and she didn't like that Hazel went on and did what she wanted, despite what anybody said. She was just like her mother, which is why my aunt couldn't stand it.

When my aunt was so excited for my pregnancy and then turned her nose up at Hazel's pregnancy, I was hurt for my cousin. How could you celebrate one and not the other? Despite the circumstances of both pregnancies, we were both blessed to bring children into this world. That was a reason to celebrate about in the first place. Often, I wished my parents were here to witness this with me. My father would have loved Grand. They were looking over me and smiling because I had got it right this time. It took a while and a lot of mistakes, but I think I finally found the right one. My baby was going to be born into a home with a lot of love. I knew Grand had another baby mama and she couldn't stand me. Grand broke up with her a week before we got together. She was the main reason I refused to live up in the big ass house he had. The bitch threatened to do a bunch of shit to me and I didn't feel safe.

"What you over there thinking about?" Grand brought me from my thoughts. He had a way of deterring me from worrying too much. It was as if he knew that I was freaking out in my head and calmed me down by removing me from my thoughts.

"I was thinking about us. I'm just so happy that we're together, having a baby and have a home together." It was true. I was the happiest I've been since my parents passed. Grand was sent to me by my parents.

"You know I have to go back and spend time with my other seeds, right?" It was the price I had to pay for loving a man that had kids out of state,

"She needs to let you have the kids for a couple weeks. I don't mind keeping them while you work."

"Nah, Tasha already in her feelings about us. I'm not trying to piss her off."

Sitting up, I screwed my face up and stared at him. "What the fuck you mean you're not trying to piss her off? Fuck her!"

"You keep trying to come in my life and stir up chaos. I don't need that shit right now. If I need to play nice to see my kids, then that's what the fuck I'm going to do. You can either get with it or become one of the baby mama's I gotta play nice with."

"Fuck you, Grand." I got off the bed and left the room and went into the living room. Grabbing my cell phone, I went onto the balcony and called my cousin. I didn't have many friends, and the ones I did didn't want to be bothered because they thought I was going to ask them for something.

"Hey, are you alright, Alicia?"

"I'm good. Just irritated with Grand. I wanted to see if you wanted to meet up or something?"

"Uh... I guess when can do that." She stalled for a second. We didn't hang out so I understood why she stalled before answering.

Not to mention, anytime I wanted to meet up with her, I was asking her to borrow something.

"Cool. I'll set something up this week for us to hang and do some shopping. Anyway, how are you and how's the baby?"

"I guess the baby's fine. I haven't been back to the doctor to check on it."

"You should definitely go and check on your baby. How's you and Denim, did you speak to him yet?"

"Um, well we did more than talking." She grew quiet on the phone. "We flew to Vegas and got married," she announced while laughing. As I listened to her tone, she was happy, and I could hear it in her tone.

"Married? Girl, you should have told somebody. What did auntie say?"

"She wasn't there."

"Your parents are going to flip. When are you going tell them?"

"I don't know yet, but I'll tell them soon as I get back home from Vegas. Alicia, please keep it to yourself," she begged me.

"You know I got you. Well, congratulations and we need to get together, so we can have a little wine celebration. You know you can have some while pregnant, right?"

"Of course, you would know about that," she giggled. "Hope you fix everything with Grand and stop being a brat. I'm about to head to dinner with Denim and his brothers," she told me.

"Denim and his brothers been fine all they life. Remember Jean? That man can take my virginity over and over again," I reminisced about Denim's older brother. That man was fine as hell and could get it anytime he wanted it.

"Um, Denim's my husband now, and I'll fight you," she giggled. "Let me go get ready because my husband is side eyeing me hard," she laughed.

"Enjoy y'all. See you when you get back, cousin."

"For sure." She confirmed and ended the call.

Sitting my phone down on the table next to the patio set, I sighed in frustration because my kitty was wet thinking about Jean's fine ass. He was fine as hell with dark skin that glistened as if he showered with coconut oil. His strong chin was covered with a thick ass beard, and he stood around 6'7 and weighed a good two-hundred and fifty pounds. It had been a while since I saw him, so he probably put on more muscle. He owned a gym in the city that was always filled with celebrities. I called myself trying to join when I was single to get close to him and canceled before they could charge my card. One month was equivalent to a month's rent. Yeah, it was nice, and all, but a bitch wasn't about to pay that.

"My homie just hit me, and I been waiting for her ass to hit me up to speak business, so I'll be in later," Grand opened the sliding door and peeked his head out. "Stop starting shit over nothing. If that's how it's going to be, I'll leave and head back home."

"Do what you gotta do." Part of me wanted to apologize and tell him I was sorry. The other part of me was like fuck it. I already had the meal ticket in my stomach, the fuck I needed him for? On the other hand, I wanted us, and I wanted us to work and prove everyone wrong. Hazel was being supportive about my relationship. Still, I knew she was waiting for it to fail like all the others. I wanted– no, I needed this to work between us.

"I'm not even stressing you. Give me a kiss so I can get gone." Standing up, I stood on my toes and kissed him on the lips. He bit my bottom lip and held it his grip on it while I pulled back and tried to push him away. He finally let it go and I stared at him like he had lost his mind. "Stop playing these little girl games with me. You gonna learn I'm not the one." He pointed his finger at me and left out the door.

I could taste the blood on the inside of my mouth as I questioned myself what the hell had just happened.

13

Yoshon

"Who is calling you in the middle of the night?" Golden stirred from her sleep and passed me my phone. We had just finished fucking hours before and were on opposite sides of the bed. Wiping my eyes, I slid my finger across the screen and put the phone on speakerphone. I was tired as fuck and didn't know what the fuck I was doing. All I wanted was for this phone to stop ringing.

"Yo."

"Yoshon, I'm in labor and about to head to the hospital with my boyfriend," I heard a voice come through my phone.

"Ight, let me know how much they gonna charge for the wheel," I responded and placed the phone back down on the nightstand.

"Huh?"

Golden shot up and shook me violently. "She's in labor, babe. Yashleigh is about to be born!" Golden screamed and climbed over to me to grab the phone. "Em, he's sleep talking. Text me the hospital and I'll make sure I get him there." She took charge as I was trying to grasp what the fuck was happening. The way Golden put the pussy on me, a nigga was fucking dead to the world. Right about now, I didn't know what the fuck my long ass name was.

"Wait, give me a minute," I responded. Don't ask me why I needed a minute because a nigga was stuck on stupid.

"Yoshon! You're about to become a father," she shook and slapped the shit out of me. "Wake the hell up!" she screamed in my ear.

"Golden, if I hit women, I would have knocked your ass out for screaming like that in my fucking face. What the fuck happened?"

"You serious? You don't know what happened?"

"Nah."

"Em is in labor and heading to the hospital. Your baby girl is on her way," she announced and my stomach dropped.

All these months and I was about to become a father in a few hours. My baby girl was about to breathe her first whiff of air. This shit had a nigga's stomach in knots as I ripped the blanket off my body and got up to grab some clothes. At this point, it didn't matter what the fuck I threw on because I was going to be a father. Yashleigh wasn't going to remember what the fuck I wore when she came into this world. All that matter was that I was there when she entered it.

"I got the keys, come on," Golden was already dressed. She had on pajama pants, a nightgown and a pair of flip-flops. I couldn't talk about her because I had on basketball shorts, a pajama shirt and some sneakers on.

"Yo, my heart feels like it's about to come out my chest," I admitted as I held the bedroom door open for her.

"Yep, that's the fresh feeling of parenthood," she giggled. "You got this, don't be worried." She smiled and assured me.

Pit Pat was waiting in the kitchen for us when went to pass the kitchen. "I heard everything. I've said my prayer for the baby and your surrogate. Call me soon as she sticks her head out that woman's hooha!" she demanded and reached up and kissed me on the cheek. "You're about to become a daddy, baby." She smiled and kissed me once more.

Golden broke all types of laws driving to the damn hospital. She was on her phone texting with Em as I was sitting still in this front seat. It was like I was staring at myself out of my body. Maybe I was in shock. For the life of me, I didn't know what I expected. I knew this is what I wanted and was happy when Em got pregnant. So why the fuck was I sitting here like I was stuck on stupid or something?

"Thank you, sir." Golden rolled the window on my side up. We were at the hospital and pulled up to the valet service. Before she got out, she grabbed my face.

"Yoshon, I know you probably feel like you have to shit, and you can't breathe. We gotta face the fact; your baby girl is coming into this world today. I need you to snap out of this and handle this like you would anything else."

"Ight, ight, ight," was all I repeated and got out the car.

We rushed into labor and delivery, and they brought us to Em's room. She was hooked up to machines and was looking like she was ready to go. "I didn't want to worry you, but I've been in labor all day. I wanted to do labor at home around my family and friends until it was time to check into the hospital," she explained and then gripped the side rail of the bed.

"The doctors say she's ready to push. They're getting everything ready and she's going to be ready. When she went to bed, she was around 4 centimeters and woke up in a lot of pain," her boyfriend explained to me.

Emily had told me that she wanted to labor as much as she could at home. She tried to convince me to allow her to have it at home and I refused. I wanted this birth to be done in a hospital.

Just because she was all into this holistic and natural shit didn't mean I had to be. The one thing she did ask was to labor at home surrounded by her friends and family until it was time to check into the hospital, so I allowed her to do that.

"T...thank you, man." I touched his shoulder. The grip I had on his shoulder was to make sure my ass didn't fall the fuck out.

"Daddy finally arrived. Well, Dad, we need to go and get this baby out. She's ready to greet the world," the doctor came in with a team of nurses. The little crib shit was waiting with all the blankets and ink shit for the baby's footprint was all laid out. Her little hat was sitting right there and waiting for her to come out so she could place it on her head.

"Okay, we need to clear this room out. Two people are allowed to be in here," the nurse said as she placed some more blankets down.

"Babe, you got this." Golden hugged and kissed me on the lips. She turned and started out the room.

"Nah. Pete, you been there and shit, but I need her in here with me."

"Dude, you got it. We've been through this plenty of times, so you know I got you, man." He hugged me and left the room.

Tears clouded Golden's eyes as she stood at the door. "Baby, I can't do this shit without you. You with me?"

With tears streaming down her eyes, she walked over and hugged me tightly. "More than you'll ever know," she whispered.

"Alright, let's have this baby. My ribs are killing me!" Emily screamed out and held onto the bed.

Golden rushed to her side and held her back up and her hand. "I'm here," she told her and smiled at her.

"I really could have used you for my other births," she joked and then her face turned sour from a contraction.

"Alright, with your next contraction, I want you to give me your all," the doctor instructed her and she did as she was told.

This was my first time witnessing a birth and my dumb ass

chose to stand in front of it all. I wanted to see my baby girl come into the world. My stomach was fucked up watching it, but when I saw the hair that wasn't Emily's pussy, I got excited.

"Babe, it's hair! She got a head full of that shit!" I shrieked in excitement.

"Oh man, you gonna be putting little ballies into her hair," she joked and continued to coach Emily from above.

"Emily, she's right here. Give me three me big pushes and she'll be out," the doctor told her and Emily pushed.

"Ah shit, her head is out!" I screamed. As Emily pushed, more of her body came out and half of her body was out of Emily's pale ass pussy.

"One more huge push and she's out."

"I'm fucking trying!" Emily cried out as she pushed so hard that her face was beet red. She took a quick breath and then did it again. A bunch of fluids and Yashleigh came out of her. They placed her on Emily's chest and cleaned her off. I was amazed seeing someone give life. The shit was nasty, yet it was amazing too. Women were fucking amazing, and if I ever doubted them, I would never do it again after witnessing what I did tonight.

"Time to cut the ambilocal cord, Mr. Santana." The doctor handed me the scissors and I cut the thick ass rope that connected Emily and my daughter. The shit almost felt final, like I was cutting her out of my life. As if she did her job and I didn't need her for anything else.

"Let me clean her up for you, one sec," the nurse said and rushed over to the crib shit. She cleaned her up, placed Vaseline on her eyes, took her measurements and then came back with her wrapped like a baby burrito. "Nine pounds, six ounces... Here's your daughter," she smiled.

Accepting the baby, I was scared as shit. I was trying to hold her correctly. She was a fat ass burrito. Who would of thought Emily's grass eating ass would have an almost ten pound baby. I sat down and held her in my arms and stared down at her. Water fell right onto her eyes and I looked up at the ceiling.

"The ceiling isn't leaking, you're crying," Golden softly spoke in my ear as she sat on the arm of the chair. "She's beautiful, Yoshon," she rubbed my back.

Yashleigh looked exactly like her mother, Ashleigh. Yeah, I saw a little bit of myself in her, but I saw the majority of her mother. She had her mother's curly brown hair, the dimple in her cheek and a widow's peak. All of her mother's unique facial features she had inherited. The shit made the tears fall faster and faster down my cheek.

"Yo, she look just like Ashleigh," I said as I held my daughter with one hand and fished in my pocket without the other one. Pulling up a picture on my phone, I handed it to Golden.

"Omg. She looks exactly like her mother. Man, her mother's genes are strong," Golden held the phone next to Yashleigh and snapped a picture with her phone. "I'm sending this to Pit Pat," she told me.

"Let me see," Emily asked as she was getting stitched up. Apparently, Yashleigh had ripped her some. "Oh wow. Science is so beautiful, isn't it? I believe she was in this room with us."

"I do too," Golden added.

"Yashleigh Golden Santana," was all I said and both Emily and Golden stared at me confused.

"Are you serious?" Golden questioned as she stood frozen in place. "Babe, you don't need to do that."

"Nah, I have to. I wouldn't have been here if it wasn't for you. If my daughter has half the strength you possess, I'm good with that. Even if we don't work out in the end, I can never think about my daughter and not you."

"You make me sick. Got me in here crying and shit," she sobbed.

"Want to hold her?"

She nodded her head and accepted the baby from me. "Hey

pretty mamas," she cooed to her. "You're so lucky to be blessed with the daddy you have. He's going to spoil you so much and tell you no a bunch of times, but he'll eventually tell you yes. Plus, you look like your mommy, so how could he tell you no in the first place?" she walked over to the windows in the room. "He'll tell you all about your mommy and I'll even ask him to tell me about her, so I can tell you stories too. Your mommy loves you so much, notice I don't say loved. She loves you and I know as you get older, you'll be confused because she isn't here, but she loves you so much. If she could be here, she would have kissed you a million times." Yashleigh smirked in her sleep. "It looks like you're already playing with your mommy. Tell her we send our love and promise that you'll never know what it feels like to be sad, alone or hurt. Long as you have Yoshon as your daddy, you will never know what those things are." She held her up and kissed her on the forehead.

Sniffling came behind from me and one of the damn nurses was crying her eyes out. "I'm so sorry. I've delivered three babies today and this by far was the most emotional one for me." She sniffled and wiped her eyes.

Golden handed Yashleigh to me and I kissed her on the lips. My daughter was finally here. Long as I had air in my body, she would never want for anything. I officially lived my life for her and for her alone. Never would anybody lay a hand on her curly brown head. One day, she would sit as the queen of the Santana cartel. Yashleigh Golden Santana was destined for greatness.

"We did it, Ash," I smiled and kissed my daughter for the second time. "We did it."

14

Golden

IT HAD BEEN a month since Yashleigh was born. We were back in New York, and everything was moving like before, except we had a newborn baby that kept both me and Yoshon up in the middle of the night. The doctor said he recommended two months before Yashleigh was able to fly because of the germs. Yoshon chartered a plane and had them clean it twice before we entered it. Once we landed, we headed straight to the emergency room to see if she was fine. I told him it wasn't necessary, but he was a new father, so I understood. The doctors told us she's fine, as long as she didn't come from out the country, we shouldn't have any worries. Any little cry and Yoshon was running across his bedroom to the bassinet to make sure she was fine. It was so sexy that he was so worried about his baby.

"I got it," he groaned as he tried to get out the bed. I was sitting beside him on my laptop writing a book. I was so into reading different authors that I decided to give it a try myself. At night seemed the best time to tune into my thoughts.

"Lay down, I got her," I told him.

"Nah, I g—"

"You're grabbing a empty bottle," I called him out and went to grab Yaya up. I gave her that nickname. "Look at you, wide awake. You like to vamp with me, huh?" I kissed her cheek and headed downstairs to make her a new bottle. This was her third bottle tonight and Yoshon tried to do feedings himself. I guess he felt like she was his reasonability and didn't want to ask me. I've already grown attached to Yaya, so I fought him on it. Just because she was his daughter didn't mean I couldn't help him out.

"Mom, is Yaya up again?" Gyan wiped the sleep out of his eyes.

"Yes, did she wake you?"

"A little. Is she okay?"

"Yes, she just wants to be held and eat. Come on, let's get some warm milk." I took him by the hand and went down the stairs. Yaya's bouncer was on the counter from early, so I slipped her right inside of it.

I made her a bottle and heated Gyan some warm milk. "Thank you, mom."

"You're welcome, baby," I said as I cradled the baby and fed her the bottle. She was sucking it down like she hadn't ate at all today.

"Mom, I always wanted to have a little sister, now I have one." Gyan smiled. He loved helping with the baby. Soon as he came through the door from school, he was excited to hold her and love on her. Yaya was truly the apple of all of our eyes. Pit Pat would sing and cook with her on the counter while I wrote and Yoshon couldn't start his day until she smiled and exposed her chin dimple. The way this man baby talked with his daughter was cute and hilarious at the same time.

"Baby, you know that Yash—"

"And Yaya always wanted a big brother, and now she has one," Yoshon's deep voice cut me off.

"We're like one big happy family," he gleamed. The smile on my son's face was priceless. To him, his world was complete and nothing or no one mattered.

"Thank you, baby," he pecked me on the lips as I fed Yaya. "Look at daddy's bugga boo," he cooed at her.

"She's so greedy," I giggled. "Acting like a little piggy who hasn't ate today."

"All her little ass do is eat. Y'all gonna come down for a midnight snack and not wake me?"

"Boy, you were trying to feed the baby an empty bottle. Your midnight snacks go straight to my butt and thighs; I'm good with some water."

"Shit, who said you can't have ribs for a snack?"

"I can find a bunch of people who would disagree with you." I placed the bottle down and put Yaya over my shoulder and burped her. Right away, she burped like she usually did. Gyan finished his milk and we headed back upstairs.

Gyan kissed Yaya and I tucked him in and placed a kiss in his forehead. "Love you, Mom."

"Love you too, baby," I smiled and closed his room door slightly. When I got back to the room, my laptop was put up, and Yoshon was in the bed smirking. "Oh no, I'm not being nasty tonight. You been wearing my ass out all week."

"You right. Put the baby in the bed and come lay down with me," he told me and I did what he said. Yaya was asleep in my arms for the walk upstairs. She would be asleep until around four in the morning. By then, I would be sleep and Yoshon could do that feeding. This little girl had me with bags in my eyes from all the night feedings. I was going to start keeping her butt up during the day so she could sleep through the night.

"She should be asleep for a few hours. I bought the bottle up and put it in the bottle warmer. When she gets up..." my voice trailed off because Yoshon covered my lips with his.

"Stop talking about the kids for a second. You always talking about what the kids need and not about yourself. I want to know how my woman is doing, how she feeling and what's on her mind?" It was weird to answer that question because no one ever asked me that. Since Gyan had been born, I had been handling things, and no one ever asked me how I felt? When Yoshon asked me, it was so foreign to hear.

"I'm fine. I've been working on a book about my life. Well, not about my life, but it's based loosely on my life."

"Word? You gonna get it published?"

"I don't know. It's something I'm playing with right now. Other than that, I've been checking on your businesses, and they're good. The tanning salon got a bad review the other day so I—"

"Golden, I wanna know about you, not my business. I want to know how you are doing, not anybody else, baby."

"It's hard, Yoshon. No one ever asks me that so I don't know how to answer it."

"Get used to having to answer that question. I want to know what's going on with you and how you're feeling. You're not here to just raise our babies and help me run my business. You here as my sex slave too," he joked, but I missed all of that with what he said.

"*Our?*"

"Yeah. Shit may seem like we're moving fast, but what's fast to others is our own pace. I'm about to be thirty-nine next month. I'm not trying to play these little cat and mice games with these women out here. I got something real staring me in my face. I don't believe in coincidences, so I believe I was meant to cross paths with you that night."

"I believe that too. I'm just so scared to love you. Loving you has the ability to destroy me if things go left."

"Good thing we're both right-handed," he made light of the

situation, as he always did when he knew I was about to get emotional.

"I'm serious. Our kids are involved. Yaya doesn't know anything yet, so if we split, she won't even know the woman she's named after. With me? Gyan will question what happened to you. You're one of his favorite people. I have everything to lose if this doesn't work out."

"Your problem is you're so busy worried about what you have to lose. What about me? I'd lose another woman that I love and someone who loves and cares for my family like it's her own. We both stand to lose a lot if this doesn't work out. I don't get into shit to fail, and this isn't an exception. When I told you I loved you in California, I meant that shit. You got baggage? So what? I got arms to help you carry that shit. Long as you got me, I got you, baby."

"You don't know how much I love you, Yoshon. I've never felt like this about someone. The way you make me feel is unexplainable. When you have to go handle business, I'm waiting until I hear your car pull through the garage. I just love being with you."

"Oh, you finally admitting you love me?"

"Shut up, stupid," I hit him with the pillow. "Yes, I love you."

"I gotta tell you something." His face became serious.

"What? Are you okay?"

"Yeah, I'm good." He started to explain to me all about his family's cartel that he had just found out about. I listened to everything he said and didn't past judgment. Yoshon never did come out right and tell me what he did for a living. I pulled the pieces together and figured it out myself. Here he was telling me everything that I had already knew.

"Wait what?" I blurted.

"I gotta go stay in Belize for a month or so to learn shit."

"You're going to actually take over?"

"Yeah. I have to."

"Babe, this is what your family decided, not you. From how you describe it, Pit doesn't even want it to happen."

"She doesn't, but she knows that I have to step up and take over. My uncle is in his seventies and wants to step down."

"I don't know. What about Yashleigh? What if something happens to you?"

"My uncle took over when he was twenty-five. You just heard me say he's in his seventies," he nonchalantly told me.

"You live in America, not Belize. It's different here," I panicked. I had finally got me a good man and didn't want someone taking him away from me. This whole cartel talk had me worried and I didn't want him to go through with it.

"How I move will have to change and shit. This is something I'm not asking your permission on. I have to do it and there's no way I can decline. All I want to know is that you'll be right there beside me and if something ever did happen to me, you would hold Yashleigh down?

"Without a question." I stared into his eyes. "I still don't like this."

"Baby, God's blessing all the trap niggas," he chuckled and I rolled my eyes. I couldn't stand this man. In this serious moment, he found a way to cause me to laugh and forget why I was worried in the first place.

"You make me sick."

"Nah, I make you in love... I didn't forget you said you love me," he pointed out and I rolled my eyes.

"How long will you be gone for Belize?"

"How long we'll be gone? Probably a month or two."

"We? How do you expect me to uproot Gyan to a foreign country for two months? Babe, I don't know about this. And what about Yaya? She's a new baby traveling out the country."

"Chill, mother hen. We'll get Gyan's tutor to come, and Yaya will be fine. I'm gonna make sure she's straight."

I sighed some and relaxed. No matter what, Yoshon was going

to do what he needed to do. As his woman, he took my feelings into consideration. Still, he was going to do what needed to be done. I didn't complain because I knew this man would never make a move that could end up hurting us. Everything he did was for his family, so I didn't expect anything less. If me and the kids had to follow him to Belize, it was something that I was prepared to do. I could work and check on his businesses anywhere, and Gyan had a tutor we used in California that he loved, so I made a mental note to call and ask her if she was available. In the end, my man was going to take the role of being the head of his family's cartel. I had to be there for him, and if it meant me getting a stamp on me and the kid's passports, then so be it.

15

Hazel

EIGHT WEEKS. I was eight weeks pregnant and didn't know what the hell to do. The little tiny thing had a heartbeat and it was strong too. That thing in there sounded like it was going to come busting out of my stomach. I couldn't believe something so small could sound so large. The nurse had to keep assuring me that it was my baby and nothing was wrong with the baby. Denim was all smiles as he held Tailor and she tried to grab the machine the lady had in her hand. The moment was special, and if I wasn't so freaked out and my anxiety wasn't through the roof, I would have appreciated it more. Since we got back from Vegas, it had been back to business. We had things that we needed to handle with the baby and me getting the rest of my things from Yolani's house. We hadn't spoken since I left the house after she pulled the gun out on me. She didn't know I actually went and got real married. This time, it was official because we got the certificate sent to us in the mail.

"You don't just go and do things without your best friend," Mo brought me back to reality as I did her nails. She had a date tonight and I had to make sure my girl was looking good. Lately, she had been dating one particular man that kept a smile on her face. Seeing her with a smile fixed on her lips did something to my soul. Mo had this glow about her recently that just set my soul on fire. She refused to bring him around and I understood. She didn't want to jump the gun yet, and I respected that about her.

"I'm sorry for the tenth time. I've been back a month and you're still bumping your gums about it." I pulled on her hand.

"Every time I see that damn rock on your finger, I'm reminded of what your sneaky ass went and did."

"It...It just happened. I'm not going to lie; I was scared. Not that scared that causes you not to do something. The scared that you get when you want to do something, but don't want to mess it up."

"Oh, that's how you know this was meant to be. Did you tell your parents yet?"

"No. They're coming over to the apartment to have dinner with us. Denim told his mother and she was so damn excited about both the marriage and baby."

"Your mother didn't question why she was going to Denim's apartment?"

"She doesn't know it's his apartment. She thinks it's mine and we're having dinner tonight as a housewarming. She tried to get out of it three times."

"Your mother loves you, Haze."

"She sure has a funny way of showing it. I just want to get this out so I don't feel like I'm hiding something from them. Despite if she approves or not, I'm happy about it."

"I could tell. You come into work every morning with a smile on your face. Denim is making you real happy over there."

"Shut up," I giggled.

It was true. Denim was making me happier than I had ever been. He sent me flowers for no reason at all, had my bath running when I came through the door from work and brought me lunch when I wasn't expecting it. This man did things that I had never witnessed in my entire life. He made me feel like a queen whenever I was around him, and when I wasn't around him, he called and checked on me. Marrying him was the best thing I could have ever done, and no one could convince me what I did was wrong. We did things our way, and I wouldn't change a thing about what we did. God was funny with the way he blessed us. Everything I wanted, he handed to me in the wrong order. The pregnancy was the first thing and now being married was the second. The things I wanted didn't happen on my terms; they happened on when he decided I needed them.

My baby, business, and husband were all that I was concerned about these days. I didn't do anything except head to work and then back home to watch Netflix and lay under Denim. Tailor had gone back to California for a few weeks until her mother went on vacation again. It was her birthday this time, and she was going on a cruise in Europe for a month. Me, as a mother to be, couldn't see myself being away from my child that long. Then again, my child was still inside of me and not running, crying and throwing tantrums, so I understood. While she was gone, she was going to be staying with us. It was going to be more practice for me. Tailor was still in diapers, so I got plenty of practice when it came to changing those.

"When are you going to get the rest of your things?"

"I know I need to call her and talk, but I don't want to. Part of me wants to leave that shit there, but some of my family's memories are there, and if I don't take anything else, I need to grab those."

"Yep, that doll your grandmother got you when you were a baby is there too."

"See, so this is why I have to suck it up and just go and talk to her. Enough time has passed, and I think we can have a conversation together without it being heated."

"No, I think you can have a conversation without it being heated. Do I think she can? No, I think she is still harboring some feelings about how you both ended. I mean, you ended years of a relationship almost instantly."

"Mo, stop trying to make me feel like the bad guy. Wouldn't you end a relationship if you found out you weren't legally married, and your husband also had a coke habit, not to mention pulled a gun on you?"

"Woah, wait!" she pulled her hand and I pulled it right back. "You didn't tell me that she pulled a gun on you. Hazel, promise me that you won't go to the house alone."

"Nobody didn't need to know that. I'm here, right? Yolani wouldn't hurt a fly. She loves to act tough, but once saved a fly I was trying to kill in the house." I giggled. Yolani was harmless and I wished Mo understood that.

"Promise me, Haze." She made me promise her I wouldn't go there alone. Mo was dramatic and I knew Yolani. I knew she wouldn't hurt me, and I trusted she wouldn't. Even if we couldn't be together, we were friends and I wanted to continue being her friend. Whatever she was going on, I wanted to help her through it. She didn't need to go on a downward spiral; we could get the help she needed now.

"I hear you, Mo. What color your annoying ass want?"

"Orange, please. I got this bomb dress that has orange in it," she perked up and left the subject alone.

Baby, we gotta postpone the dinner tonight. I gotta catch the red-eye to California tonight. We got an investor for the business and he wants to meet tomorrow morning.

I saw the message that came through from Denim. I was angry because I knew he had to handle business. Shit, I was relieved because I hadn't pulled anything out the freezer to cook tonight. My mother wasn't thrilled about tonight in the first place, so she would be excited that she didn't have to come over.

Babe, business comes first. Handle yours.

Nah, you come first. I'll see you before I head to the airport. Love you.

Love you too.

"Heifer, don't be stopping my nails to go and text your hubby back. Get to doing what I'm paying for."

"Um, Mo, you don't even pay me so shut the hell up." We both broke out in laughter. With how much Mo did for me around here, she wasn't allowed to dig in her purse and pay for anything. I covered her nails and I was the only person allowed to do her nails. My friend came through for me so many times, and if doing her nails so she looked bomb on her date was the least I could do, it was as good as done.

Me and Mo stuck around and chatted for a bit before she had to run and grab the kids to take to the sitter. Once she was done, I shut the shop down and headed home. I was tired as hell and just wanted my bed. While chatting with Mo, I sent my mom a quick text, and she told it was fine, and she was tired anyway. I knew she didn't want to come and the sad part was that it didn't bother me that she didn't want to come. Keeping this secret from her felt food. It was like I was keeping a piece of happiness for myself without her being negative about it. I sat in my car and look at Yo Yo's nail sign and sighed. I remember when Yolani surprised me with this shop. She had evil ways about her. Still, she had a heart so big that I didn't know how it fits in her chest. You had to know her to witness that side of her. We didn't have all bad times. There were more good than bad. Except the bad was so bad that it ruined the good times we had. The things she has done to me was stuff I couldn't forget.

Before I knew it, I had pressed her name and the phone was ringing. It rang a few times before she answered the phone. "Yo."

"Hey."

"What's good?" her tone was dry. Yolani was more emotional than what she let on. She liked to act like she was tough and bad. In reality, she was a big emotional mess.

"How are you?"

"Chilling. You know how I am. What about you?"

"Whew, a lot. I think we need to sit down and talk. Enough time has passed and we're friends before anything else," I was the first to bring up what we both spend this conversation avoiding.

"Shit, I'm free whenever. Let me know."

"I need to come grab the rest of my things, so I'll come by there if you don't mind."

"Cool. When?"

"Tomorrow afternoon, good?"

"Said I'm free whenever," she repeated.

"Okay. Cool."

"Bet." She ended the call quickly and I held the phone to my chest. While she thought I was happy about this, I wasn't. Yolani was my best friend. Fuck the whole fake marriage; this was a woman that had been a friend to me before we got together. Anytime I needed something, she was there for me and never complained. I just wanted my friend back more than anything. I wanted my friend to be alright and to get cleaned. Yolani needed to be right for herself before she thought of a relationship with anybody. Right now wasn't the time for her to be focused on someone other than herself. When I met up with her tomorrow, I was going to be sure to mention her getting clean. I wanted her to know that I was going to be there for her through anything. I loved her and wanted the best for her. Wiping away a tear, I put my car in park and pulled off toward home. You couldn't want more than someone wanted for themselves. In the end, I had a child and a husband I had to worry about. We both had different priorities now.

You GOT THIS. Just get your stuff, talk and then leave. If she doesn't want to help herself than there is nothing you can do except say a prayer and go on about your life. This is what I went over in my head as I stood at the front door of the place I once called home. Yolani came from the den, where she always was, and opened the door. The glass window in the front door allowed me to see where she came from. She was dressed in basketball shorts, tank top and Nike slides. Her hair had seen better days; her nose was red as an apple and eye pupils were dilated. It didn't take a scientist to know that she was high as hell. Something told me to come back and do this later, but seeing her face made me walk through the door.

"You got here quick." She smirked and walked behind me. "Damn, that ass got thicker," she licked over her gold teeth.

"I had to go the post office and forward my mail, so I was in the area. What's been going on with you? Pit hasn't been over here?"

"Nah, she and Yoshon pissed with me right now. Nigga over there playing house with that bitch Golden and won't even let me see my niece."

"Huh? Niece. Golden's pregnant?"

"Nah, he had a surrogate carry one of Ashleigh's eggs. He kept the shit a secret and just told us when the baby about to be born."

"Oh wow. I have to go over there and see everyone."

"For what? We not together anymore, or are we?" she held my hand up and stared at it. "Nah, you handed me my ring back, fuck is this ring?"

Snatching my hand back, I held onto my purse and thought of a way I could tell her that wouldn't hurt her feelings. "I got married, Yolani."

"Married? Stop fucking with me." She walked into the den.

Following behind her, I spoke. "Me and Denim got married last month. It wasn't planned and it's something I wanted, he didn't force me to do anything."

"You went and married that square ass nigga. The only hard part about that nigga is the dick he was putting in you behind my back. Fuck boy ass nigga."

"You have your right to feel how you do. I shouldn't have been sleeping around when we were together. It wasn't right and I'm sorry about it."

"Fuck all that shit. You blamed me about all the bitches I fucked, and you were out here fucking and doing shit behind my back."

"I'm going to get my clothes and stuff. I'll grab as much as I can and come back another day." Right there in front of me was three lines of coke ready for her nose to devour.

"Yeah, do you. Shit, you been doing you."

Heading upstairs, I went to my closet and grabbed what I could. I placed some in suitcases and made sure I grabbed the most important stuff first. My doll from my grandmother, family pictures, and important documents. It broke my heart that she was in the big house alone and stuffing her nose with drugs. The shit made me sad and upset because she should have wanted better for herself. Except, she wanted to be a loser and do drugs. Why couldn't she deal with her issues without going to drugs? The fact that Yoshon wasn't dealing with her meant he found out about the drugs. Yolani looked up to her big brother. To hear that he wasn't deal with her and keeping his first child away from her, I knew that shit was bothering her more than she was letting on.

"Up here taking all the shit I bought you?" she cackled and stood in the doorway. "Just going to come in the crib I provided for you over the years, tell me you're married to the nigga you was cheating with and take the shit I worked hard to provide." Her voice was low and callous. It was eerie listening to her talk as she leaned in the doorway.

"I love you, Yolani. Loved the hell out of you and wanted to be with you. You did everything wrong and then continued to act like it didn't matter. You didn't fight for us. Why do you want me to fight for something you weren't even fighting for yourself?"

"I gave you everything you wanted. Love, I gave that shit to you more than I gave to anybody else. What the fuck did you want from me? I tried, this shit ain't no damn textbook, I didn't know what the fuck to do. All I knew is that I love you and wanted to make this shit work with you." She walked closer with tears in her eyes. "I still want to make this shit work with you. This house... Nah, my life ain't the same without you. I had the best intentions when I married you, baby."

"We can have the best intentions and still fall short," I wiped away the tears that fell down my cheeks. "I'm happy, Lani. For once, I'm so happy I don't know what to do with myself. I don't want to make you feel like shit, but I'm choosing me and my child. Me and Denim are having a child and it's all I wanted from you. I had to realize that I was being selfish by expecting you to give me things that you didn't want. For so long, I relied on you to make me happy and I realized that I was wrong. I needed to make myself happy before someone else could make me happy. Yolani, I love you and will always love you, but we can never be together. I love you, but I love myself more. I choose me this time, not you." I was hysterically crying as I stood in front of her. She looked so hurt and broken.

"Y...you're pregnant?" she stuttered.

"Two months. I just want us to remain friends. I don't want to cut you out of my life for good, but for my child I'll do it. Yolani, you gotta get clean, this isn't you," I begged.

Grabbing my suitcase and duffle bag, I walked by her. I knew she wasn't ready to change, even after losing me and having her family not talk to her. This was something that Yolani would have to fight alone. I couldn't want this more than she wanted it for herself. In the end, I wanted her to get clean, but if she didn't want that for herself then there wasn't anything I could do. As I made my way toward the steps and started down them, Yolani came out the room.

"So that's it? You walk in here, in the Versace leather jacket and boots I bought you and think that you can tell me you're married and pregnant? That's what we doing now, Hazel?"

"I told you what it was. Get some help. I don't want this life for you. Despite how we ended, I want you to be happy." I turned and walked down the stairs. I felt a hand on my back trying to push me and I held onto the banister. "Stop, Yolani. What the fuck are you doing!" I screamed.

"I leave bitches, not the other way around." She pried my hands off the banister, put her foot in my back and kicked me down the flight of stairs. I went tumbling down the stairs and landed on the bottom landing. I couldn't feel my body and tears slipped down my eyes. I was dizzy and everything was swirling around me.

"I see what the fuck Bruno was talking about when he said Versace on the floor." She snarled and stepped over me. The last thing I heard was her sniffing some coke into her nose before everything faded to black.

To Be Continued
No questions this time, just sound off in the reviews. I want to hear what you guys have to say!

www.facebook.com/JahquelJ
http://www.instagram.com/_Jahquel
http://www.twitter.com/Author_Jahquel
Be sure to join my reader's group on Facebook
www.facebook.com/ Jahquel's we reading or nah?

Part Three Is Coming 06/29!

Bless our page with a <u>Like</u>

Part Two Is Coming! Catch Up On Part One Now!

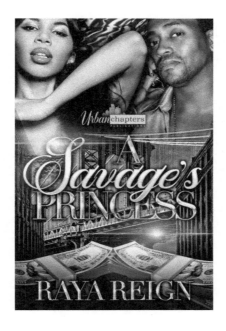

The First Of The Coke Gurls Releases This Month!

Coming This Month!

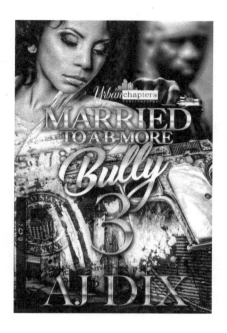

CPSIA information can be obtained
at www.ICGtesting.com
Printed in the USA
LVHW05s1947200618
581394LV00021B/318/P